Rise of the Elite

A compilation of personal log entries, interviews, stories, and memories by
J.C. Stevens

For Janet

My soulmate and the love of my life. Thank you for being the Godly woman who encourages me, cheers me on, and prays for me. Words alone cannot express how much I love you.

Prologue

Everyone has milestone dates in his or her life. These dates can represent times of celebration like birthdays or anniversaries, but they can also mark dates of tragedy and loss. We purposely remember the good days and are sometimes haunted by the bad ones. As much as we try to anticipate and avoid the bad days, they come; often they come by surprise.

Tom Marshall was a senior government monitor, and he was the best of the group. It was his job to monitor the elite - those who appeared to live normal, happy lives but were born different than the rest of us. They were unique by design but standardized for the safety of society. He often said the job felt a lot like being a spy but without the international travel or fancy gadgets shown in the movies. It fascinated and consumed him. Tom completed a thorough psychological analysis on every one of his clients, recorded their every move, and covertly set them up to live in the most stable environment possible. He had access to medical records, school records, profiles and just about anything else that could possibly be required to monitor and document their lives.

Originally, the monitors were each assigned one client. After a few down-sizing efforts to save money, they all had to take on more. Soon, they were all monitoring four or five at a time. Clients were divided by geographical location, but it was still a lot of travel and a lot to keep up with. The time investment required was immense.

Every doctors visit, every fender bender, every vacation had to be monitored. Oftentimes it was necessary to intervene in order to steer their lives away from danger or risk. Intervention was not always an easy task since so many of them were kids, teenagers, and young adults. It all had to be done without them knowing. Clients had to keep believing that their lives were normal just like everyone else. When one of them made a sudden change in behavior or routine, it was up to the monitors to document and analyze the event. Every risk was anticipated, avoided, and logged. The data had to be detailed and intimate. The risk of missing something carried potentially severe consequences for society. The monitors thought they were flawless; their systems were perfect. They thought they had everything under control. They were wrong.

Chapter 1

Tommy's favorite childhood memories were the days he spent with his grandfather. It was a simpler time back then; at least it seemed so to Tommy. His grandfather owned the only mechanic shop in their small town just north of Tallahassee Florida and Tommy would often stay at the shop on the weekends to help Grandpa clean tools or sweep the floor. Grandpa Marshall loved a clean shop; he said it made a better impression on his customers.

Grandpa always opened the shop early because he wanted to be ready for customers when they needed him. He enjoyed being able to spend the mornings watching the sunrise with his only grandson. Most of the rest of the day was spent replacing a car part or trying to find the solution to an elusive problem. Grandpa Marshall never gave up when he was faced with a problem.

Tommy admired his grandfather. Although, at ten years old, Tommy was too young to understand what the word "integrity" meant, he knew that his grandfather had it. Grandpa Marshall was in his early sixties and had been running the mechanic shop for the past twenty years, after he was laid off from a local manufacturing plant. He was very muscular for his age and had a head full of grey hair that was often marked with car grease. He wore the same dark blue coveralls every day, except for Sunday when the shop was closed.

The shop had three bay doors and a small office on the east side of the building with a desk and two chairs where Grandpa Marshall would keep up with the paperwork required for running his business. For as long as he owned the shop, at least two of the three bays were always filled with cars or trucks that needed attention. Tommy loved to play in and around the shop. The only piece of equipment that frightened him was the vehicle lift that came out of the floor and raised the cars up over his head when Grandpa was working on them.

"You stay out from under those cars unless I am with you, okay Tommy?"

"Yes sir," Tommy replied.

Many of the days at the shop are indistinguishable from each other in Tommy's memories, but there is one day that stood out above the rest. It was a Saturday afternoon when Miss Peterson drove into the parking lot of the shop and walked into the small office. Grandpa Marshall noticed her arrival as he popped his head around the open hood of a car he was working on. He set down the wrench he was holding, grabbed a towel to wipe the grease from his hands, and started walking to the office to meet her. Meanwhile, Tommy was playing with a magnet and some

4

small metal balls Grandpa had taken out of an old bearing. When he saw Grandpa Marshall move toward the door, he hurried to his side.

"Did you hear that Tommy?" Grandpa Marshall asked as they walked together.

"Hear what?" Tommy responded mimicking his grandfather's motions.

"The noise Miss Peterson's car made when she parked her car."

"No."

They walked toward the office, and Grandpa smiled as if he already knew what the problem was. He politely held the door for Tommy to enter first and then followed, still rubbing the grease off his calloused hands.

"Good afternoon, Miss Peterson," Grandpa Marshall said as their eyes met. She looked flustered and guilty. She was a single mom in her early thirties, and she frequented Grandpa Marshall's shop to keep her worn car in decent running order. She responded in a quiet, sheepish tone as if she had been caught doing something wrong.

"Good afternoon. I know I should have brought it in sooner. The noise started several weeks ago, but I had to wait until my next pay cycle and..."

"It's okay Miss. Peterson," Grandpa Marshall replied, "It sounds like the bearing in your alternator is bad. It is a pretty distinctive noise."

"How much will that cost?"

Grandpa Marshall walked over to the filing cabinet that sat behind his desk and opened the third drawer as he continued speaking.

"If I remember right, we replaced that alternator less than a year ago. I think it still has a manufacturer's warranty on it that will cover the replacement."

Grandpa Marshall emerged from the filing cabinet with a piece of paper that showed the purchase and warranty information on the alternator.

"Are you sure it is covered?" Miss Peterson asked, "I thought it had been more than a year."

"I'm positive, Miss Peterson. The paperwork doesn't lie. I'll check it to make sure I'm right. With a thirty-dollar labor charge and a couple of hours, I can get you back on the road by the end of the day."

Miss Peterson was relieved to hear the news. She was expecting much worse. Grandpa Marshall had always treated her, and all his customers, with fairness and respect. She handed him the key to her car and told him that she would be back in a few hours. As she left, Grandpa Marshall looked down at Tommy with a smile on his face and the paper still in his hand.

"One of the secrets of a successful life is to work hard and keep good documentation," he said as he set the paper down on his desk.

"Isn't that two secrets, Grandpa?" Tommy responded in a puzzled tone.

"Yes, I suppose you can count that as two, Tommy,"

Tommy seemed to soak up every word his Grandpa told him. Grandpa Marshall pulled an old stethoscope out of his desk drawer that had been modified for a mechanic's use and started walking to the front door.

"You stay in the shop Tommy. I'm going to take a quick look at Miss Peterson's car."

Tommy ran out the door to the shop and back to the spot where he was playing with the magnet and balls. As he reached for the makeshift toys, one of the balls dropped to the floor and rolled underneath a car that was raised on the lift. Tommy knew he wasn't supposed to go under any car or truck that was raised on the lift, but he convinced himself that it would only be a second. He tiptoed under the car slowly and carefully. He reached down to the floor to pick up the ball and then stood back up. Tommy breathed a sigh of relief when nothing bad happened.

Tommy reached up to touch the bottom of the car engine. Grandpa never let him touch anything when they were under a car. The oil pan felt smooth and cold. He felt confident that he had conquered his fears about the lift and that he had proven himself worthy of being there all by himself. His confidence quickly grew to over-confidence, and he kicked one of the front legs of the lift just to show his dominance. As he retracted his leg from the kick, his foot snagged on a metal wire near the beam of the lift.

Tommy was shocked when the lift responded back. He heard a popping sound and he froze. His eyes were wide, and his pulse was quick. He tried to steady his breath when suddenly he heard a creaking and the snap of metal. The car over his head shifted. Tommy dropped to the greasy floor as the sounds of metal scraping metal filled the walls of the shop. His eyes were filled with horror as the car started falling toward him, moving as if it were in slow motion. He was paralyzed with fear. Tommy cried, closed his eyes tight, and held his breath. Suddenly, he heard his name and opened his eyes.

He looked up to see Grandpa Marshall kneeling with both arms up holding the engine. The rear of the car had already fallen almost to the ground. Grandpa Marshall's muscles bulged as the sound and the motion of the car stopped.

"Go," he said as he strained to keep the front of the car in the air.

Tommy scurried out from under the car. As he passed the rear tire, he turned around to look into Grandpa's eyes. They both stared at each other in amazement for only a fraction of a second. Amazement instantly turned to panic as Grandpa Marshall suddenly realized the weight he was holding. The look of panic on his face was burned into Tommy's brain as Grandpa's arms and legs both buckled under the weight of the vehicle. The mass of metal came crashing down and echoed both in the shop and in Tommy's head.

The rest of the day seemed like a blur. Tommy's parent came to pick him up, and the police barricaded the shop. Tommy refused to eat for days. For the next few weeks, Tommy's parents dealt with closing out the affairs of the business and dealing with a tragic family loss. Tommy had to tell the story so many times that he finally learned to tell it without breaking down in tears. Family and friends were amazed at the heroism and supernatural strength Grandpa Marshall displayed to save Tommy's life. Several of them congratulated Tommy for being brave, but he didn't feel brave; he felt responsible.

Every second of the ordeal was burned into Tommy's memory, and for the next few weeks he would replay the event in his head over and over again. Months and years passed quickly but he could still remember every vivid detail of that fateful day. As he grew up, Tommy was drawn to read about similar stories of extraordinary strength in times of duress. He was fascinated by the untapped capability of the human mind and body.

The incident with Grandpa Marshall was the first time Tommy had ever been exposed to something supernatural, but it wouldn't be the last.

Chapter 2

Many years passed and Tommy grew up to become just "Tom". He excelled in school and graduated at the top of his class at West Point Military Academy. He was handpicked for a classified government job and was trained by the best. As the years passed, he became one of the strongest agents in his twenty-year career as a government monitor.

Compiled here are some of Tom's personal journal entries and pieces of the story as he told it to me. Eyewitness accounts and my own creative freedom fill in the blank spots of Tom's story. I believe his story is worth telling. The impact he had on my life and the life of my family will never be forgotten.

Tom was a field agent and could only be found occasionally in his Atlanta based office. On a particularly warm day in April, he was sitting at his desk working through one of the many reports that needed to be complete. Everything in his office was kept tidy and labeled. The layout was so efficient that it became the standard for every government office in the building. Desks were always centered in the middle of the room and perpendicular to the wall with the door and hallway window. Behind the desk were rows of black filing cabinets and a high-back black leather business chair. In front of the desk were two rigid chairs designed to be uncomfortable for long visits. His workspace was clear except for his spare computer monitor and a thin layer of dust that usually settled on the surface when he was out in the field.

George Miller was Tom's boss. He was a tall, slender black man with a small hump on his back from years of slouching. Around the side and back of his head he had a ring of grey hair; it was all that was left of what he described as a lush black afro at one time. George's fashion sense was dated by about ten years, but he always looked professional. No matter how warm the weather, he consistently walked in the office every weekday in a long sleeve shirt and tie. By lunchtime, the tie would be hanging on the coat rack behind his door and the sleeves of his shirt would be rolled up to his elbows. George usually topped off his attire with a grin on his face that he maintained all day long. He was a great office manager and everyone in the department respected him. When George was somber, everyone knew something was wrong. April 24th was one of those days George was solemn. He skipped his usual loop around the office area that morning to greet all the agents at their desks and, instead, walked straight to his office and closed the door behind him. Tom noticed the break in George's traditional routine as he kept working on his report, and he took special note of the unusual behavior to record in his personal log at the end of the day.

Tom Marshall Monitor Log Personal File APHL37

Today seemed like the start of any normal day, but it wasn't normal for me; it was a day of loss. I never talk to anyone anymore about the tragic loss of my grandfather so many years ago, and I likely won't tell anyone about the loss I experienced on this day as I make this file entry, but in some strange way, it gives me comfort to write it down. Perhaps it is the nature of my job to document significant events, or perhaps it is just my way of coping. As I write this entry, the words of my grandfather haunt me – *work hard and keep good documentation.*

This morning, after spending an hour of solitude in his office, George walked into my office with a grim look on his face and simply said, "Tom, I need to see you in the conference room. I need to talk to everyone."

He left as suddenly as he had appeared, leaving no time for questions or conversation.

I could tell by the look on his face that the news was not going to be good. I paused for a moment with my fingers frozen still on my keyboard as I watched George make the rounds to all the other offices personally inviting everyone to the meeting. I was mid-sentence in my report, but George's brief visit left my train of thought completely blank. My corner office had a great view of the hallway leading toward the conference room near the back of the building. He visited every occupied office on the hallway stopping only to request attendance to this mysterious meeting. It was unusual for so many of us to be in the office, but we had all been called in from the field to be available for an important announcement. It was a big deal to pull everyone in on such short notice. The rarity of the event led to a great deal of paranoia and speculation about what was happening.

Jeff Rogers sat in the office next to mine. He had trained under me since he started with the agency and was very young and excitable. Jeff was also the office fashion diva. He wore the latest style slacks with perfectly matching dress shirts and a different pair of Italian leather dress shoes every day. He was always clean shaven and could have gotten a night job as a magazine fashion model if he wanted to. I didn't have hard proof, but I was certain he spent most of his paycheck on clothes and hair gel. Jeff looked the part of a government agent, but under that façade, he was a nervous wreck. Any minor problem that he encountered usually became a major event that required several of the more tenured agents to intervene. Jeff kept a stash of antacid in the bottom drawer of his desk. He was only twenty-six years old but had the ulcers of a stressed-out old man. After my brief visit from George, Jeff came half-running into my office completely panicked.

"Tom, what's going on?" he asked as he sat down quickly in the chair across from my desk and immediately began tapping his pen on the arm of the chair. "Is this another down-sizing? Are we losing folks again? I have already taken on more than I can handle, Tom. I can't afford to lose this job." Jeff rambled on for a few minutes as I kept my eye on George through the window, making his rounds. I was asking myself some of the same questions but decided to keep a calm and peaceful demeanor. I had to pretend like everything was under control. So many of the younger folks looked up to me; if I started panicking, chaos would ensue.

By the time George made it all the way down the hallway, I had completely tuned Jeff out. He tended to over dramatize everything. On any given day when he was not in the field, Jeff could be found at the water cooler or in the break room complaining about how busy he was. I suppose he was trying to convince everyone in the department, including himself, that he had the drive and initiative it took to be successful. George had been very patient with him, much more than I would have been. If I were in charge of the department, I likely would have fired him months ago.

If I had let him, Jeff would have sat there rambling on all day. "Jeff," I interrupted, "let's go see what this is about."

"Right, Tom," he replied putting his pen in his pocket as he stood up. Before he could get to the door of my office, he started biting his fingernails. If we were downsizing again, my vote would have been for Jeff to go. His nervous habits and constant whining were just overwhelming.

I tolerated Jeff because I was assigned to train him when he started. He worshipped me by trying to follow every move I made and adapting my strategies as his own. As much as I tried to build the passion within him that I had for this job, he just didn't have what it takes. He wasn't willing to sacrifice like I did. He wasn't willing or able to focus on doing the job as his top priority in life. His lack of initiative was disappointing to me, but the way he idolized me alleviated some of my frustration. As annoying as he was, he helped elevate my ego.

There had been a drastic change in training over the years. When I was recruited into the department, we were trained in mechanics, physics, biomedical technologies, anatomy, and psychology. Anything that could possibly be needed to handle a potential upset situation became a requirement for us to know. Over the years the training requirements diminished significantly. Jeff and the group that came in with him were nothing more than glorified administrative assistants. It bothered me to an extent, but it gave me an advantage when George did performance ratings, so I didn't complain about it.

"Listen Jeff," I said as we walked out the door of my office, "showing signs of panic is weakness, and that isn't what we get paid for, is it? It is our duty to protect society. To do that, we need to show some resolve and be willing to do whatever it takes. That is what makes people great." Jeff nodded in agreement still biting on his nails. I was thoroughly impressed with my own tidbits of wisdom that I could pass down to the younger generation. I dare not let him or anyone else know that I was just as clueless about what was going to happen. Jeff was convinced that I had the inside track, and I saw no good reason to change that impression.

As we both walked down the hall to the conference room, Ben caught up with us and gave me the probing look. "Any idea what this is about?" he whispered.

"We'll just have to wait and see", I replied softly, "but it's probably not good news." Ben started with the department two years before Jeff's group, and he was the polar opposite of Jeff. He was quiet and reserved. Ben was in decent shape for a young man, but his face had held on to his childhood baby fat and freckles, making him look much younger than he really was. Ben didn't report to me directly, but he did contact me periodically for advice. He was a hard worker, but he stuck to a nine to five schedule that left him in the dust against folks like me who were willing to sacrifice a bit more. Like any organization, improvement requires sacrifice and meetings, like the one we were all going to, usually meant more sacrifice on our parts. With years of dedicated service behind me, I wasn't afraid to sacrifice more; I just detested not knowing how much they were going to ask of us.

Chapter 3

Tom Marshall Monitor Log Personal File APHL37

(cont.)

I entered the conference room where George had already taken the seat at the head of the table. It was unusual to see him so visibly upset. He had been with the department since its inception. In my twenty years with the department, I had only seen him shaken up like this once before. George cleared his throat, as my remaining co-workers made their way to their seats.

"Well folks", George said, "as many of you have guessed, I have some bad news." The room was completely silent. Even Jeff sat still as everyone stared intently at George. "The nation's economy continues to be in turmoil. Our new president is taking some drastic measures to curtail government spending, and that means closing down some non-critical departments."

George paused for a moment. I could tell that he had rehearsed this announcement all morning, but it seemed as though it just wasn't flowing like he wanted. After a deep breath, he continued, "We are one of those departments". As soon as those words left his mouth, the room was filled with sounds of discontent and questions that George was unable to answer.

"Listen," George said trying to regain control of the meeting, "I need everyone to go back to your desks and start organizing your files. There are still some field agents that I need to contact, and then I will meet with each of you individually to discuss future options. We have until the end of next week to clean house. Thank you for coming."

George was so diplomatic about clearing a room. We all knew those final words were his closing statement, and it was clear that the meeting was over. One by one, everyone started walking slowly back to their respective offices with downcast faces and grunts of despair. I was in shock. I stayed in my chair as everyone else walked out. Not wanting to express my disbelief in front of the group, I just sat there staring at George. Once the room was clear, I started pounding George with my thoughts.

"George, what's really going on? This can't be the end. They need us. Surely we can just cut back a little bit and..."

"I'm sorry Tom, it's over;" George interrupted. "They're shutting down our department completely and permanently."

"That can't be right George. What if..."

"Tom, we're done; the decision is final. There is nothing more we can do now." George wouldn't look me in the eye. I could tell that he was struggling to maintain his composure. The words seemed difficult to express.

I paused, still in disbelief.

"What are we going to do? This is all I have."

"Listen Tom, this isn't going to be easy for anyone. For folks like us, it changes everything we know about life. The only thing we can do is accept the hand we have been dealt and move on. I have a job waiting for me at the FBI. I can put a good word in for you if you want."

"No," I said, still in shock. "That's not what I signed up for. This is the job I want."

"This job is gone," George said finally making eye contact with me. He got up and started to walk toward the door. "I'm sorry, Tom. We all need to move on." He put his hand on my shoulder as he walked by. I imagine it was all the encouragement he could muster on a day when he was forced to crush the lives and careers of those he managed. I stayed in the conference room for a few minutes. The room was vacant and quiet, but my mind was full and deafening with thoughts of disbelief.

We had gone through some downsizing and restructuring just like every other government department in the past, but I never thought they would shut us down completely. I suppose our new president just didn't see the value in keeping us around. Our job was to ensure there were no incidents with the elite, and we did our job well. I suppose we did our job too well.

I sacrificed everything for this job; it was the only thing I had left in life that brought me any satisfaction. I pushed myself so hard so early that I just didn't have any time left for family, friends, or social events. The thrill of my career became the only thing important to me. I loved the research, the secrecy, and the prestige of having high level government access to any place at any time. It totally consumed my focus and my life.

After years of arguments with my parents over priorities and life choices, we finally just stopped talking; that was so long ago. I would have thought that the years of learning the "value of work" from my father would have made him proud to see me embrace commitment and loyalty to the department. Instead, he did nothing but chastise me for investing so much in my job. I was on a critical assignment in Pennsylvania when they died in a car accident. I never got the chance to make things right with them. The timing was terrible, and I couldn't even make it to their funeral.

My short marriage ended in divorce fifteen years ago. Her name was Victoria, and she was the most beautiful woman I had ever seen. At first, she was excited about a relationship with a top-secret agent. We both thrived on that excitement and rushed headfirst into marriage. We were together less than a year before the reality of my career demands weighed too heavily on our relationship. She couldn't handle the travel and secrecy required of my job. I couldn't share with her the details of my day at work. I couldn't explain the last-minute trips or the frustration that I felt in recording the lives of other families while seemingly throwing my own life away. Too many nights, I left her alone and longing for some level of conversation or company. It was just too much for her. She did everything she could to make it work, but I was so consumed with work and her solo efforts just weren't enough to salvage the relationship. The truth is that she deserved better than me. She realized that fact before I did, and by then, it was too late to change it. Our marriage died quickly and within just a few short weeks the divorce was final, and I was alone again. Regret lasts a long time.

For years I had no friends. I had no family. I had no life outside of my duty. And now, after twenty years of dedicated service, there was nothing to move on to. The department had become my family and the elite had become the focus of my life.

Closing the department was a mistake. Why couldn't they see it? Without our department in place, something was bound to happen. The risk was far too great.

Monitoring, data collection, analysis and intervention were all done with the upmost precision and without any suspicion that there were deeper things going on behind the scenes. As I reflect on the past twenty years, the job was a series of thankless tasks and work to direct the lives of the elite to pursue safe, normal environments for the safety of society.

Sometimes watching their little league games or Christmas programs made me long for something more in my life. Maybe if I had chosen to get out sooner, I could have saved my own marriage. Maybe I could have had a family, too. By the time those regrets crossed my mind, it was too late to fix any of it. I had a job to do.

Although I had some regrets, the truth is that I loved my job. It made me feel important. It made me feel like I played a huge role in keeping the world safe and that I was making a difference. When George told me the news, I felt lost. This was all that I knew. I suddenly found myself in unfamiliar territory as a forty-three-year-old unemployed special agent. I knew my job was important. I knew that the world needed me to protect them. The politicians didn't understand that. They didn't know what was at stake. This was all just a political game to make them look better for cutting government spending while still giving themselves a nice annual pay raise. They didn't care about the risks. All they wanted was cost savings so they could advertise how well they were doing and keep their jobs with their plush offices and pretty homes.

And now, despite all my efforts, my dreams just vanished before my eyes. Today's loss brought back so many painful memories. I didn't know what else to do than to write it down. Today made me feel like nothing I had done in my life mattered. I just wasn't needed anymore. I was alone and left with an insignificant severance package, an uncertain future and time. I had plenty of time.

Tom Marshall Monitor Log Personal File APHL37

End of Record

The environment of the department changed that day. There were no more smiles and no more jokes. George did his best to try to find placement for everyone, but there just weren't enough jobs. Tom's disbelief and bitterness made him unwilling to accept anything other than what he had been trained for. He tried to maintain a good game face, but it tore him up inside.

Tom spent the next several weeks taking his complaints all the way up the leadership hierarchy. He tried to warn them about the risks, but they just wouldn't listen. He even offered to take a pay cut, but there was no room for negotiation. The decision had been made. Technology had allowed the elite to blend in with society. As the risk of danger subsided so did the need for the monitors.

Chapter 4

The elite were categorized by ability. There were enough of them in the system to accurately profile and rank them. The class categories were based on risk. Those with a higher skill profile also had more associated risk and were categorized as Class 3. Moderate skills correlated to the moderate-risk elite were categorized as Class 2. Low skills were associated with low risk and were categorized as Class 1. The tenured folks like Tom were always given the Class 3's. If anything ever happened the situation could quickly become very difficult to contain and control. Class 3 elite required much more attention, and the monitors had to predict and direct their lives to keep them safe. Tom was the only one in the department that could handle five Class 3's and several Class 2's simultaneously. No one else was willing to invest the time.

The elite were always transferred to the department when they were little children. Each one had a file with their projected ability profile, family tree, background, social status, and temperament category. The department kept the files up to date with any changes or additions.

The program started roughly forty years ago. John was the first of the elite. He was born a perfectly normal and happy baby boy in Dallas, Texas. John's parents were a middle-class couple just getting their family started. They read all the books and took all the classes to be the best parents possible. John was definitely worth the time and effort. He was born with a head full of black hair and chubby cheeks that drew the attention of every grandmother in the city. The first year of his life was nothing out of the ordinary. He babbled, sat up on his own, crawled around the house and filled every diaper that was put on him. His parents were thrilled with their little boy and they gave him everything he needed to be happy and healthy. John was on track with his development progress and was considered average by his pediatrician. Medical testing, though, cannot predict everything; John was certainly not average. Just after he turned one year old, John broke out of his crib, literally. His parents took him to the best doctors and specialists, but his condition was unlike anything they had ever seen. John's muscle mass and the density of his skin structure were developing far beyond any normal growth measures. There wasn't a car seat or highchair that would hold him.

The details behind what was different about John were kept classified. Some speculated it was all the hormones that had been pumped into food over the past several decades. Some quoted Oscar Wilde's essay about life imitating art in a society enamored with comic book superheroes. Regardless of the cause, it seemed to be limited to the United States, and the medical scientists of the time soon discovered a proliferation.

John had some abnormal brain development that gave him extraordinary abilities. By age two, the government had moved John and his family to a secluded research facility at a top-secret location. Video files that showed John breaking through brick walls and concrete blocks without a scratch on him were shown only to a select few. It was amazing. They had special programs to restrain him and regulate his abilities for their testing purposes only. The researchers were amazed and frightened at the thought of the things John was capable of. John suffered through a mirage of tests, needles, and probes. After months of testing and documenting this amazing child, the unexpected happened. Something changed. When he was three years old, John had a sudden massive brain hemorrhage and died. John's parents were crushed. They were compensated generously by the government for their loss and for their continued confidentiality regarding their son. The strain of the experience tore their marriage apart. They were divorced shortly after returning to Dallas. John's mother was so distressed that she took her own life a few weeks after the divorce. John's dad took the government hush funds, left the country and, according to the rumors, made some solid investments and became a multi-million-dollar philanthropist.

Julie Monroe was the second known elite. She was the first child of Robert and Suzanna Monroe. The Monroe's lived on a little farm just outside of the small town of Griffin, Georgia. Their little fifteen hundred square feet red brick house was set on a picture-perfect country dirt road. Robert was tall and muscular with short brown hair, brown eyes, and a charming smile. The farm had been in his family for generations, and his heart's desire was to raise a family of his own while keeping the farm alive and profitable. Suzanna was an attractive young lady with short bouncy blond hair and rich blue eyes. Robert and Suzanna were high school sweethearts. They were married shortly after their high school graduation and wanted to start a family right away. They struggled for a few years trying to have a child and, after spending all that they could afford on vitamins, medicines, treatments, and doctor's visits, they had almost given up on their dream.

Four years after they were married their dreams were revived as Suzanna walked out of the doctor's office with a smile so big that Robert said it blinded him from the opposite side of the waiting room. Eight months later, they were able to finally hold the baby girl they had prayed for. Julie was a very content baby. She rarely fussed and seemed to learn quickly. Although they weren't wealthy, Robert and Suzanna gave her everything they could possibly afford. By the time she was two years old, Julie was running around the farm in overalls and sandals with her long blond curly hair bouncing in the breeze and a sparkle in her big brown eyes. She was anxious to discover all that life had to offer.

Julie had a wonderful imagination and, on any given day, could be found dressed up like a fairy or a princess granting wishes to her subjects who generally consisted of the local farm animals, also wearing their princess best.

Julie's unique skills were a little more difficult to detect early. She was a healer. When Julie was three years old, Suzanna twisted her ankle on the front steps of the house while walking out to get the mail. The pain was excruciating, and she fell to the ground grasping her injured foot with both hands while the tears flowed. Julie had never seen her mommy cry like that. Julie's face was downcast. Her bottom lip puckered out and her own eyes began to water. Julie did the only thing she knew how to do; she hugged her mommy and insisted on kissing her boo-boo as she had seen her mom do to her on several occasions. Julie squatted and held her lips to her mom's ankle. She kept her mouth on Suzanna's ankle as if her lips were stuck to her skin. After a few seconds, Suzanna began to feel awkward sitting on the front step with her daughter attached to her ankle. Slowly and steadily her entire foot grew warm and flushed. Julie then stood up and said, "I love you mommy. Please don't cry." Within just a few minutes, Suzanna stood up on the front walk and stared at Julie, confused and amazed. Her ankle was warm and throbbing, but the pain had subsided, and it was strong enough to stand on.

"I love you too, sweetheart," she said wiping the tears from her face, "let's go back in the house."

After putting Julie to bed that night, Robert and Suzanna had a long talk about the incident but had no idea how to handle it. They decided to treat it as a fluke circumstance and to not read too much into it.

Suzanna was a skilled homemaker, but she was prone to clumsiness. Her lack of grace led to another demonstration of Julie's ability several weeks later when she accidentally cut her finger in the kitchen. Suzanna immediately dropped her knife in the sink and began to wash the fresh wound mumbling to herself about how clumsy she was. As she stood over the sink trying to stop the bleeding, she stopped and glanced over her shoulder to see Julie playing in the living room. "Julie," she said, "please come here." Julie obeyed immediately and came running up to Suzanna, grabbing the back of her legs in a tight hug. "Look honey," Suzanna said with a certain level of curiosity in her voice, "Mommy cut her finger."

The cut wasn't very deep and had stopped bleeding but was red and slightly inflamed. Julie looked intently at Suzanna's finger, grabbed it with her little hand and said, "Sorry, Mommy." Suzanna felt the warmth of Julie's touch, and the pain stopped.

Just as she had done before, Julie paused with her little hand grasping Suzanna's finger. They both stood silent. Suzanna wanted to believe that Julie could heal her finger but was afraid of her daughter being abnormal. The opposing feelings battled inside her as she felt her injured finger throb. Suddenly, Julie was distracted by the sound of the television in the other room. She let go of Suzanna's finger and ran back to her toys. Suzanna immediately pulled her hand up to her face and saw that the cut was gone. A small faded white scar remained where the open wound had been. Her whole hand was red as if all the blood in her body was fighting to fit inside the blood vessels within her hand.

When Robert came home Suzanna explained everything that had happened that afternoon. At that point, they both knew that there was something special about Julie, but they decided to keep a low profile and continue watching her in an effort to maintain a normal life.

Julie grew up in a very loving family. Her parents were hardworking and honest. They were amazed at her abilities but never used them for their own gain; they had too much integrity to do so. They consistently used life as moments of opportunity to teach Julie how to do the right thing.

As she grew, Julie learned how to use her ability to heal others. Julie had a big heart and wanted to help everyone she saw. Robert and Suzanna often had to hold her back so she wouldn't attract too much attention. She was prone to simply walk up to a stranger in a wheelchair and strike up a conversation.

"Hi, my name is Julie", she would say. "What is your name?" Her innocent demeanor and adorable smile always solicited a friendly response. "Why are you in that chair?" she would ask. "I can help you stand up, if you promise to keep it a secret". She always made them promise, and they always did. Julie wanted to save the world one person at a time. She was perfectly poised to be a world-changer. Robert and Suzanna did their best to find the balance between letting Julie help others and keeping her abilities out of the public spotlight. The struggle often kept them up with late night discussions about ethics and morals. A forcing factor in their decision came sooner than they expected.

Chapter 5

When Julie was six years old, the government found her. Someone had not kept Julie's secret, and soon the Monroe family had government agents knocking at their door. Julie and her family were immediately quarantined from the rest of the world for research, and her abilities became the government's secret to hide. The Monroe's were removed from their farmland and were set up in a secure monitored facility in Virginia. Robert tried to oppose the move, but he was no match for the government scare tactics. They convinced him that this was all in the best interest of his daughter, and he reluctantly conceded.

The government science experts of the time had great hopes that enough research about Julie's abilities could cure many of the terminal illnesses that plague society. Unfortunately, none of that research was realized. At the age of seven, Julie passed away. Her death was both sudden and similar in circumstance to John.

Robert and Suzanna were devastated. They had always dreamed of having a large family. They had tried to get pregnant for so long before they had Julie, and they cherished every minute with her. Now their little girl was gone. They moved back to Georgia to surround themselves with a familiar environment and try to move on with life to the best of their ability. There were no words to describe their anguish. The loss and the heartache they felt marked a turning point in their life. Although Robert and Suzanna's loss was similar to John's parents, they committed to stay together and work through their anguish hand in hand. Though broken-hearted and grief-stricken, they found some level of comfort in a local church and made a concerted effort to use this tragedy to strengthen their relationship. Robert refused the government offer of financial compensation for their loss believing that it disrespected the cherished memories of their daughter.

Ultimately, what the scientists found was that John and Julie both had a unique DNA abnormality that triggered a level of specific brain activity never documented before. Soon after the discovery, the government took swift action to ensure the test for this type of DNA variation was included in the normal prenatal testing for all babies across the country. Since the establishment of the National Medical Network, tracking the records was all too easy, and the elite could quickly be identified prior to their birth.

The elite were categorized by ability, and soon doctors and scientists were able to predict what special skills each of them had even before they were born. For data gathering purposes, there were cases where the government manipulated the disappearance of some of the babies for testing. Although devastating for their families, government leaders felt it was necessary to analyze these individuals for the common good.

Those that survived became some of the first test subjects for various restraining technologies. The details of the tests and the number of test subjects was kept top secret. Tom only knew about the bits and pieces that George would tell him in confidence. When George divulged some limited information, he talked about it as though it was a time in his life where he questioned his orders and felt some regrets. Still, George was one of the charter members of the monitoring department, so Tom and the rest of the monitors held him in high respect and didn't probe where he was reluctant to share information.

The categories were established to identify the potential risk to society if the elite were allowed to fully develop. Class 3 elite were considered the highest risk and were mostly comprised of those with enhanced strength and endurance similar to John. Class 3 elite were not indestructible but often had extremely dense skin tissue and an ability to produce massive amounts of adrenaline that fueled muscle growth. Class 3 elite would be the most difficult to control if they chose to use their abilities at the cost of harming society. Within Class 3, there were different magnitudes of development dependent on body type and muscle mass, but even the lowest development level still presented a great risk to society.

Class 2 elite were gifted with a unique connectivity to other people. Some Class 2 elite, similar to Julie, could hyper-accelerate the production of white blood cells in another person's body with just a touch, bringing advanced healing to damaged tissue. Other forms of Class 2 connectivity were much more complex. Some Class 2 elite could concentrate to synchronize their brain waves with another person in close proximity, allowing them to tap into the other person's immediate thoughts. Although not viewed as a physical risk to society, these elite could easily use their abilities in pursuit of personal gain at the expense of others.

Class 1 elite were the lowest risk, comprised primarily of those with heightened senses. Class 1 elite developed with extraordinary vision or an enhanced hearing range but showed no other signs of significant abilities that could make them a risk to the general population.

The research on John, Julie, and the rest of the early ones also led to another key discovery – how to prevent the development of these abilities. It was called the restrainer chip, a tiny microchip inserted in the brain stem that would hinder the development of the abnormality. There was a great debate among the nation's top leaders to develop a strategy for handling the elite. The seemingly common premature death rate of the first few elite coupled with the potential risk of having superhuman beings integrated into society led to the mandate of the restrainer chip. Several key physicians across the country were trained to handle the implanting of the chip shortly after birth. It was a relatively easy procedure and since there was advanced notice with the prenatal tests, there was plenty of time to prepare.

Two years after Julie's death, the Monroe's became pregnant with a son. As soon as they discovered the gender of the baby during a normal prenatal doctor's visit, they agreed on naming him Jacob. Robert and Suzanna were very excited to have another baby, but the news of the pregnancy was accompanied by a haunting fear. The thought of losing another child filled their hearts with anguish. After a couple of preliminary tests, Jacob was found to have the same genetic qualities that made Julie special. He was also projected to be a Class 3 elite. Jacob was one of the first test subjects for the restrainer chip. Robert and Suzanna were ready to do whatever was necessary to save their son's life. They were asked to return to Virginia, but this time Robert insisted that they stay home. The loss of Julie had strengthened Robert's convictions about doing the right thing and taking full responsibility for leading his family.

They knew that this procedure could save Jacob's life, but they also knew the risks. They were united and firm in their position on keeping the family at home. If something were to go wrong, they wanted to spend as much time with Jacob as possible, living a normal life on their farmland. After the implant, the Monroe's were visited weekly for the first six months and then monthly to check Jacob's growth. The time commitment required to track and document Jacob's progress led to the development and organization of the monitoring department. The Monroe's case was unique because they knew the monitors were watching. The first monitors had a mutual understanding with the Monroe family and did their best to give them their privacy. In some ways, it was easier than dealing with the other families who didn't know that they were being monitored.

Jacob was Tom's first assignment. When Tom joined the department, Jacob was already nine years old and had shown no signs of abnormal growth, super ability, or side effects from the chip. Robert and Suzanna were always very cordial and often invited Tom to dinner to keep him updated on Jacob's activities. The success of the restrainer chip with Jacob quickly led to implantation with the other babies identified as elite.

Everything was kept extremely top secret. The parents of the remaining elite babies were not informed of the tests or of the procedure. When an elite was identified, the assigned physician logged and tracked development through the gestational period. Once the infant was born, they would be swept away for some "non-critical" testing and implanted with the chip. After the procedure, each of them seemed to grow up normally without any adverse side effects.

Once the chip was implanted, the elite were officially transferred to the monitoring department for tracking. The department documented everything and looked for signs of abnormal behavior or development issues. It was a flawless operation. The chip seemed to be working properly, and all of the test subjects were developing just like any other child. The chip was virtually undetectable unless there was a head x-ray or MRI. The department had some strict protocol to handle any such cases should they arise.

The monitors took on the responsibility of ensuring the integrity of the chip. Any accident that had the potential for head injuries could put the system at serious risk. There was much at stake. Keeping society safe and eliminating the risks associated with allowing the elite to fully develop their abilities was the paramount purpose for the department.

The system worked so well for so long that the monitoring department was deemed unnecessary. The elite were being tracked long before birth, and the restrainer chips were working without fail. Any incident was diffused quickly and quietly to avoid any public or media curiosity. The travel and labor costs to maintain the department were significant, but for the twenty years that Tom served, it was necessary.

All of the early monitors were exclusively picked for the mission. The assignment began as an honorable position, but after almost thirty years without a significant incident, it devolved into a burden on the taxpayers. Suddenly, the best and brightest minds from some of the most respected educational facilities in the country were transformed into just numbers in some grand government financial analysis. Tom felt betrayed by the agency

41

that he poured himself into. The weeks and months that passed after the department closed did not alleviate his frustration. It seemed like more than just a cost-cutting measure; it seemed like an attack on his pride. He couldn't help not taking it personally. He felt like he was being underutilized and undervalued. After twenty years of dedicated service keeping the elite restrained, now he felt restrained himself. Time passed, and Tom finally gave up trying to reason with his former leadership. He had no other choice than to resign his position of importance and consider his monitoring assignment as glory days of the past. He had to move forward but he didn't know what he was moving forward to.

Chapter 6

"Good afternoon, ladies and gentlemen. We will now begin boarding flight 828 to New York starting with passengers with seats in the first-class cabin," the attendant called over the sound system.

Richard Hall saved his file, closed his laptop, and headed to the gate. The Atlanta airport was particularly crowded, and the smell of grease from the fast food kiosk next to the terminal gate filled the air. One of the few people who wore classy business attire for travel, he walked briskly to the ticket agent with his boarding pass ready and a charming smile to help expedite his transition. His naturally blond wavy hair was trimmed to perfection so that it didn't move when he walked. Although he was friendly as he continued down the jet way, he was clearly focused on his work. He boarded the plane and quickly made his way to his assigned first-class seat, opened his laptop, and picked right back up where he left off. Richard always preferred the aisle seat. He felt like it allowed him to get off the plane faster and he wasn't much for gazing out the window. As the coach passengers passed by, he never even flinched. He was consumed and focused on his work.

He paused for a moment while trying to compile the perfect transition from one thought to another when he felt a pair of eyes staring at him. Richard glanced up to see an elderly lady seated directly across the aisle from him with a worn purse in her lap. She was easily in her seventies and wearing a paisley patterned dress only an older lady could get away with. She had silver white hair, fair wrinkled skin, and light blue eyes that were longing to make contact with her traveling neighbor. As Richard glanced at her, she smiled and said, "Good afternoon". Trying to be polite, he returned the greeting and immediately turned his focus to his computer. His lack of engagement in conversation didn't deter the elderly lady a bit as she made another attempt to strike up a conversation.

"Where are you off to?" she asked.

"New York City," Richard replied still starring at his laptop screen and typing vigorously. "I have a big presentation to do there tomorrow." For a few short seconds, he clung to the hope that his response would be taken as a hint to leave him alone. Those hopes were met with disappointment as she kept talking.

"New York is such an exciting city," she said. "I don't get to stay there much. This is just a connecting flight for me. I am going to Madrid. I've never really been out of the country before, but my son moved there four years ago with his wife. This will be the first time I get to see my grandson. I've never flown first class before, so this is an exciting trip for me."

He hummed in acknowledgement still trying to politely end the conversation. He kept his eyes glued to the computer screen, but she pursued the conversation relentlessly.

"What do you do for a living?" she asked.

"I am in marketing," he said, "working my way up the corporate ladder."

"Oh, how nice," she replied. "What are you selling?"

"If all goes well, I'll get this account and be selling pest control chemicals," Richard said still unwilling to glance up and make eye contact.

"Oh," she said. "Aren't those dangerous?"

"It's all in how you market it," he replied, "all about the show."

That was one of his favorite phrases. He picked it up from a professor in college and kept it handy as one of his generic responses to justify the importance of his job.

He typed furiously trying to get every last letter in before the announcement was made to "please stow all personal electronic devices in preparation for takeoff". Reluctantly, he placed his laptop in his briefcase and tucked it under the seat within arm reach. He looked back over at the elderly lady who was still smiling at him. He now had no reason to ignore her and she wasn't going to leave him alone. This was certainly going to be a long flight.

"Good afternoon folks, this is Captain James Collins welcoming you aboard flight 828 to New York. We are number two for takeoff so sit back, relax, and enjoy your flight." The words were all too familiar. Richard had grown accustom to ignoring them and was preoccupied with getting in the air so he could finish his big presentation for his meeting. At twenty-three years old, he had only worked for the firm for less than a year but had already poised himself to move quickly up the corporate ladder. His charming personality and strategic thought process were perfectly matched with his career choice.

"You know, I don't know much Spanish; I hope I'll be okay when I get to Madrid," the elderly lady said, still vying for Richard's attention.

"I am sure you'll be fine," he responded as he leaned forward and buried his head in his hands.

"Are you okay?" she asked.

"Yea, fine, just enduring a bit of a headache," he said, hoping that she would get the hint.

"Oh dear, I think I may have something for that," she said as she started digging through her purse. She paused for a minute to glance out the window as the plane turned the final corner poised for takeoff. "Here we go" she said in her overly sweet southern tone.

As the engines revved up, Richard was rehearsing his speech in his head. He leaned his head back and closed his eyes to completely focus on his presentation skills. The plane built up speed and the passengers were shaken as the plane vibrated under the force of acceleration. The nose slowly lifted, but before the rear wheels left the ground there was a loud thump near the wing of the aircraft followed by the sound of crushing metal. The overhead bins burst open causing luggage and other loose items to become dangerous projectiles. The calmness of the airplane cabin instantly became an environment of chaos. Muffled screams were heard throughout the cabin as the nose of the plane smashed back down on the runway breaking the front landing gear. The pilots slammed on the brakes and the plane began to weave uncontrollably as it slid down the runway. Richard grabbed the armrests of his seat, closed his eyes as the force of the sudden drop jerked his head forward. Shards of metal and debris flung from the aircraft as part of the wing detached. A section of the wing bounced off the ground and flew back toward the plane penetrating the rear of the aircraft. The damaged hull skidded off the edge of the runway into an open field. The interior of the plane immediately filled with smoke. The mangled aircraft came to a sudden halt throwing up dirt and debris everywhere. Several of the passengers had been rendered unconscious or worse. Those that were still conscious were dazed and in shock.

For the next few days, the headlines were filled with details of the tragic plane crash. "Flight 828 out of Atlanta crashed on the runway while attempting a routine take off...." "Waiting for exact number of casualties in the crash..." Every news station on television had a crew at the crash site stirring up media frenzy.

The amount of damage was astonishing. There was video of the wreckage, interviews with passengers and witnesses, and short clips showing a steady stream of paramedics going in and out of the airplane. Some of the survivors walked off the plane with only minor injuries including a sweet older lady in first-class while others were taken to the hospital. One of the injured but unconscious survivors was Richard.

Richard was one of the elite and one of Tom's former clients. He was young and energetic, smart, and completely in control of his destiny. Tom watched him grow up, graduate Magna Cum Lade at an Ivy League school, and start his career in business. Tom had a deep respect and admiration for Richard because of his drive to succeed. On more than one occasion, he caught himself thinking that if he had a son, he would want him to be a lot like Richard.

Tom was assigned Richard when he was twelve years old as part of a consolidation effort in the department. Richard grew up in a very affluent family just north of Atlanta. His first car was a BMW, and he had all the toys imaginable. Richard worked hard during his high school and college years and was brilliant in his strategies. He was the guy who could always be found in name brand fashions and usually with one or more pretty girls hanging on his arm. He was tall and handsome with bright blue eyes and a charming smile. Richard's perfect teeth and blonde hair made the guys jealous and the girls swoon. He had a tone, muscular body that he religiously maintained with a semi-weekly weightlifting routine at the gym. Richard had everything going for him.

Richard's father was a wealthy businessman living the American dream. His mother was a doting socialite who set the standard for young gold-diggers everywhere. They weren't bad people, but they were completely disengaged from Richard's life; still, they provided for his every need. They set him up for success, and Richard capitalized on the opportunity.

The impact of the crash left Richard unconscious and slumped over in his seat. When the rescue workers reached Richard, they strapped him to a straight board and rushed him to the hospital. The emergency room was crowded with crash victims, all being cataloged and ranked in order of priority based on the severity of their injuries. Survivors with minor injuries were being checked and interviewed. Richard was admitted quickly and wheeled off to an operating room with significant head injuries.

The plane crash left Richard bruised and battered for several days. His mom was vigilant about staying at his bedside during visiting hours. His father was out of town on business, but had his personal assistant send flowers and made sure that he was set up in a private room for his recovery. Richard didn't know that the plane crash would change his life so drastically. His restrainer chip had been shattered. The crash had left him with so many wounds that the doctors dismissed the presence of the broken chip as debris and removed it. He was lucky to survive. By the time he was discharged from the hospital, still a bit sore and shaken up, the news reporters had moved on to other disasters and the memory of the incident was already fading in the eyes of the public. They were completely unaware that the real story had just begun.

Chapter 7

Richard was profiled as a Class 3 elite. If allowed to develop, he would have had abilities similar to John. The effects of removing an existing restrainer chip in one of the elite were unknown. The monitoring department had kept such good control of the elite that the scenario had never presented itself, at least not until now.

Shortly after Richard left the hospital, it was evident that something about his body was changing. His body was healing rapidly. He felt stronger and better than ever. Without the restraining chip, his brain triggered a massive production of steroids and adrenaline. Within days, he started noticing how easy his weightlifting routine had become. Within a week, he had broken almost every faucet handle in his house.

The turning point for Richard came two weeks after the crash. Completely healed and trying to get back to the action of his fast-paced job, he was speeding down the interstate to make a nine-o'clock marketing presentation. Always multi-tasking, he had his phone on speaker, his breakfast in one hand and the steering wheel in the other. Suddenly, the flash of blue lights in his rear-view mirror captured his attention.

"No, no, not now, I don't have time for this," he grumbled to himself as he abruptly ended his phone conversation, stuffed his phone in his jacket pocket, and pulled his car to the side of the road. He glanced at his watch feeling the pressure of being late and the embarrassment of sitting on the side of the road in front of a police car with lights still blazing. It felt like the police officer was taking forever to approach his car. Richard pushed the button to let down the driver side automatic window and stared at the side mirror the entire time. Every second of waiting for the inevitable encounter increased his frustration. Finally, the officer stepped out of his vehicle and approached his car door with ticket book in hand. *It's about time,* Richard thought to himself as the officer approached him. *Let's get this over with.*

The highway patrol officer was a short but muscular man with his head clean shaven and a pair of mirrored sunglasses reminiscent of a 1980s cop television shows. He strutted up to the side of the car and Richard was temporarily blinded by his shiny name tag that read *S. Davis.*

As he glanced in the rearview mirror, he saw another police car pull off the road behind the first one. The second car had also turned on the flashing blue lights, but the officer remained in the vehicle. In early morning traffic, it was common for the police to tag-team the busy interstate, but Richard took it as a personal attack.

"Great," he said under his breath, "I've got two of them after me now."

"Can I see your license and registration please?" Officer Davis asked.

"Officer, please, I am already late for a very important meeting," replied Richard as he frantically searched for the vehicle registration.

Officer Davis was unaffected by his plea. "Son, do you know how fast you were going?" Without time for Richard to answer the officer, he also added, "You know you shouldn't be eating and driving at the same time."

"Yes, I know that" he replied, more than a little aggravated by the whole situation. "Here it is," he said.

As he turned to hand Officer Davis his license and registration, the driver's license slipped from his hand and fell to the ground. Both Richard and Officer Davis paused for a moment.

"Please step out of the vehicle, sir" said the officer as he backed away from the car door.

"You have got to be kidding me," Richard said under his breath. At this point his emotional distress was evident, making Officer Davis feel threatened and putting both men on edge. He opened the car door, unbuckled his seat belt, reached down, grabbed the license and slammed the door shut again. "Here it is, officer," he said with a hint of attitude.

"Sir, I asked you to get out of the car," said Officer Davis now standing about four feet behind the car door. His body language was guarded.

Richard became visibly flustered, "Come on man; I accidently dropped it, now I picked it up for you. Please just write me the ticket so I can get out of here." The emotional upset had become too much for the police officer to let him stay in his car. Richard's threatening tone warranted a firm repeat of the command.

"Sir, step out of the car, walk to the rear of the vehicle, and put your hands on the trunk" he said.

Richard, barely able to contain himself opened the door again, stepped out of the car and walked toward the trunk waving his drivers' license in front of his face. The officer in the second vehicle stepped out of his car and slowly approached as Richard continued his rant.

"This is ridiculous", he exclaimed. "You're making a big deal about nothing, and now I am really going to be late." Just then, Richard's phone vibrated in his pocket. His natural instinct was to reach in his pocket to grab the phone. Officer Davis interpreted Richard's hand movement as an act of aggression and, breaking his normal police protocol, immediately tried to tackle Richard to the ground. As he lunged for Richard's body, Richard turned to brace himself and flung Officer Davis across two lanes of traffic directly in front of an oncoming tractor-trailer. The truck driver immediately locked his brakes, but it was too late, and there was no time to react. Tires screeched from both sides of the road as cars collided and veered off the road to avoid being hit.

The second officer backed up and drew his weapon. He alternated between yelling at Richard and talking into his police radio.

Richard stood stunned for a few seconds. The sound of crushing metal jarred him into action. Shocked and scared after feeling a sudden burst of strength, he jumped back in his car, jerked the gearshift downward and took off. His face turned ghostly pale, and he could feel his heartbeat intensely as the knot in his stomach grew. He stared straight ahead weaving in and out of traffic trying to get as far away from the scene as possible. The cold sweat was pouring from his forehead and soaking through his undershirt. He left behind a trail of smoke, damaged vehicles, a panicked police officer, and a crowd of injured witnesses.

Chapter 8

Richard's situation soon evolved into a familiar news story. He was driving southbound on a four-lane interstate passing most of the thinning traffic. Most of the interstate entrance ramps had been closed off. Behind his black Mercedes were a dozen police cars with lights flashing and sirens blaring. Still shocked at what he had done and more than a little frightened, Richard kept replaying the whole incident in his head. His hands were cold and clammy, and his eyes were glazed in disbelief. His grip on the steering wheel was so tight that his fingers left indents on either side.

"What am I going to do?" he said to himself. "This is all just a really bad dream. This can't be happening to me." His head was flooded with questions that didn't have answers. The air conditioner was at full blast, but the sweat kept pouring from his brow. He was desperate for a way out and was trying frantically to regain his thought process.

Finally, after twenty minutes of driving in a stupor of confusion, Richard reclaimed enough of his senses to stop and try to explain what had happened, even though he didn't quite understand it himself. He slowed down and pulled his car over to the side of the road. The police quickly surrounded him with weapons drawn and aimed directly at him.

"Step out of the car with your hands up," the voice bellowed over the loudspeaker. No longer concerned with his meeting, Richard was far more compliant this time. He slowly opened the car door and moved one foot out onto the ground. He moved as though he was in slow motion. He carefully stepped out of the car with his back turned toward the police officers and his shaky hands held high in the air. His body was trembling, and his throat was dry.

"Lay face down on the road with your hands out," said the officer over the loudspeaker. By this time, the roadway was hot, and traffic was stopped both ways. Cars in the opposite lane came to a halt as drivers and passengers alike stared on. Richard slowly dropped to his knees and then lay face down on the pavement with a look of terror on his pale face. The sounds of car engines, news helicopters, and voices filled his head as he was trying to plan out his words and wrap his mind around all that had happened.

Several police officers walked slowly toward him still with weapons drawn. Richard felt the weight of one of them as they jumped on his back and snatched his hand. Another officer grabbed his other hand and thrust it behind his back as the metal handcuffs clenched his wrists. The news helicopters captured the whole event and broadcasted live. Richard was soon relieved of his phone, wallet, and pocket change and was harshly placed into the back of a police car.

As the tow truck arrived to load Richard's Mercedes for the impound lot, Richard sat with his head down in the back of a police car escorted by two officers on his way to police headquarters. Soon the news helicopters were gone, the scene was cleaned up, traffic resumed a normal pace, and the attention of the public shifted to other news stories.

"What is happening to me?" Richard asked rhetorically from the back seat of the police car.

"You killed an officer. You're going to jail for a long time," one of the men responded without looking back. His tone was straightforward and emotionless.

"I can't spend the rest of my life in jail," he pleaded. "This is all just a mistake. You have to let me explain." The car was silent. The silence didn't deter Richard from recounting the whole story in hopes of winning some pity with his escorts. The handcuffs were very tight on his wrists and his hands began to swell. "Please, I need you to listen. I need someone to help me figure this out," he begged, but the officers remained stoic. Richard twisted his arms to get more comfortable and the handcuffs snapped in two leaving him with a shiny bracelet on each arm. He was surprised that they had broken so easily, but he kept his hands behind his back so that his police escorts wouldn't notice. Again, Richard tried to plead his case with the officers. Feeling unrestricted by the handcuffs, he sounded much less panicked as he made his logical plea. "Look, this whole thing is a misunderstanding. I didn't do anything. I was just trying to get to work. Please, let me go." Again, there was no response. Knowing that they were getting closer and closer to their destination, Richard started pleading more. "I can't go to jail. I didn't do anything wrong!" he exclaimed getting more fidgety in his seat.

Then, in a moment of desperation, he turned and kicked the car door. The rear passenger side door flung off the car and landed in a ditch on the side of the road as the driver slammed on the brakes. Before the car came to a screeching halt, Richard jumped out and ran toward the wooded area on the side of the road. The officers quickly exited the car with weapons drawn yelling for him to stop. He wasn't going to jail, no matter what. Richard ran full speed into the thick brush.

He could hear the crunch of dead leaves as the police officers continued the chase through the woods. Richard kept running with sweat pouring down his face as the forest started to get thick. One of the officers was yelling at him to stop while the other was screaming into his radio calling for back up. There was no mistaking their tone; they were willing to stop him at any cost. Richard felt his heart pounding; he managed to keep a steady pace on the rough terrain while jumping over fallen branches and dodging tree limbs. The sound of the officers screaming filled his head, but he could tell that they were losing ground. Some of the brush was dense, but Richard ripped through it like it wasn't even there. The officers chased relentlessly for several minutes. As motivated as they were, the officers were no match for Richard's young physique and enhanced strength. Before he got out of range, both officers stopped and began firing their guns. He felt the sting of two objects hitting his back. The shots almost knocked him off balance and welts began to throb. Without looking back, he kept running deep into the woods until he couldn't hear anything but the sound of his breath.

With his heart still pounding in his chest, Richard glanced behind him. There was nothing in sight but trees and brush. He felt like he had run for hours. His body was warm and throbbing, but he wasn't tired at all. He slowed his pace and finally came to a stop. Richard examined his back to the best of his ability but found no blood. The areas were sensitive to the touch and slightly raised so he knew they were going to bruise, but the bullets had not penetrated his thick skin. His expensive dress clothes didn't fare as well.

Mystified and frustrated at the events of the morning, Richard paced back and forth. "This cannot be happening," he murmured to himself. Replaying the frustration he felt when he first got pulled over and the embarrassment he felt when he had to get out of the car made him more upset. The voice echoed in his head, "You killed an officer…"

"I couldn't have done that. It's just not possible," Richard continued, still pacing back and forth. Over and over again, he replayed the scene as the frustration continued to build inside of him. Finally, he let out a shout of anguish and kicked a nearby tree. The entire tree shook. The dent left in the trunk was deep. Richard's foot throbbed for only a few seconds and then felt completely normal. He examined the tree to find that it was bent over as if a car had hit it. Stunned by his own strength, he stood back, made a fist with his right hand, aimed carefully, and swung with great precision at the same tree. The sound of a mighty crack filled the air as the tree came crashing down. Richard stood silent in awe of what he just did. The trunk of the tree was larger than his thigh and must have stood fifty feet tall before he knocked it over.

He stood with open arms staring at his hands for a few minutes. The color had returned to his face as the shock and disbelief at his situation was being overpowered by his adrenaline and curiosity. Wood debris and broken branches covered the area and the smell of shattered pine mixed with sweat permeated the air. The sun broke through the trees and created a shiny reflection from the handcuffs onto his face. He slipped his finger between the handcuff and his left arm and pulled until it gave way. When he repeated the procedure for his right arm, it flew off even easier. Richard sat down on part of the fallen tree to gather his thoughts. As he examined his torn clothes, he began to plan his next move.

Get a grip, Richard thought to himself as he sat alone in the dense forest. *This cannot be happening to me. None of this is my fault. If that cop hadn't been such a jerk and just let me go, none of this would have happened. They took my car, my wallet, and my phone. There is no one I can call for help. My reputation is ruined. I'm sure the firm is going to fire me, and my parents are probably mortified. I just got shot…twice, and I have no idea what to do next.*

Richard continued trying to analyze his situation, but he was having some difficulty thinking straight as the random thoughts kept racing through his head. He tried to rationalize his situation as he rolled up what was left of the sleeves of his business shirt and removed his tie. "I need to get back into the city and I need to get a change of clothes. I need to make some sense of all this," he said talking to himself.

The manhunt for Richard in the wooded area was extensive but the authorities had significantly underestimated his endurance and speed. Richard had made it far outside of the perimeter boundary they set up and was just south of the developed area of the city. The police didn't find the damaged tree and Richard's abandoned tie until much later.

He began walking back into the city. His entire body throbbed with energy as the sound of leaves and brush under his feet echoed through the woods. Richard was making a mental inventory of people that he could go to for help. He didn't like to face problems alone. Obviously, the local authorities would already be in contact with all his relatives in the city, including his parents, so he couldn't go there. He had some friends at the firm but wasn't sure who he could trust. His safest bet was Jennifer Stokes.

Richard met Jennifer during his sophomore year in college. He was playing basketball with some friends when he landed wrong after a poorly executed jump shot and twisted his ankle. Jennifer was a medical student and helped tend to his sprained ankle. They became good friends, though she had always hoped their relationship would evolve into something more. She was a very smart girl with a great personality, but her homely complexion and straight brown hair didn't turn many heads around campus. She knew that he was way out of her league, but at least he was friendly to her. She found contentment just being his friend and his on-call nurse when he got sick. Much to her dismay, Richard took no romantic interest in her.

It seemed like a bit of a long shot, but it was the only shot he had. Richard hadn't talked to her since he graduated over a year ago, but he knew that she was still at the University. He was counting on her willingness to help him again. After his recent airline experience, Richard thought it would be best to make the drive to Pennsylvania for a visit.

64

He started feeling better now that he had some semblance of a plan in his head. He was a very task-oriented person and had already made a mental list of needs in his head when he heard his stomach growl. "Great," he said to himself. "Now all I need is a car, some money, a phone, some clothes AND lunch." While he walked, he continued formulating strategies that could get him to Pennsylvania quickly and soon found himself in the rural area south of the city and entering the urban streets of Atlanta. He had to find a place where he could get quick and easy access to cash and a car without attracting a lot of attention.

Chapter 9

Tom Marshall Monitor Personal Log File AGAL67

My cell phone rang shortly after two o'clock the afternoon that Richard had his episode with the police. I instantly recognized the number.

"Tom, it's George. There has been an incident, and we need your help." George's voice was serious, and his sentences were short. In the months since the firm closed down, George and I had only talked a couple of times. George was busy with the new job, and I was still bitter about the whole layoff situation. George was a good friend to me and tried his best to encourage me to move on with my life, but some wounds take time to heal.

"What's wrong George?" I replied, "What's going on?"

"Are you in a place where you can talk?" George asked.

"Yes, what happened?" I replied.

"It's Richard Hall," George continued. "Somehow his restrainer chip has malfunctioned and now we have a serious problem on our hands."

I stifled my desire to say, "I told you so" and listened carefully as George described the events of that morning.

"We have police dash-cam footage of Richard throwing a patrolman across two lanes of traffic and killing him. He snapped a pair of handcuffs like they were paper, destroyed a police cruiser, and fled into the woods just south of Atlanta. We raided his house but haven't found any conclusive evidence regarding what may have happened to his chip. The damage in his apartment indicates that he may have been dealing with this for a couple of days. Tom, I don't have to tell you that this is a potentially dangerous situation. I have been commissioned on a team to bring the situation under control, and I need your help. Can you come down to the old office building immediately for a full debriefing?"

"Of course, George" I replied, "I am on my way now. I will be there as soon as I can". I grabbed my wallet and keys and raced to my car. The adrenaline was rushing through my body and for the first time in a long time, I wasn't dwelling on my painful past.

As soon as I got to the building, I headed straight for my old office. When they closed the doors, they left everything right where it was. The furniture in the office had a thick layer of dust from sitting undisturbed these past few months. After a brief pause of breathing in the musty air, I walked straight to the filing cabinet, pulled Richard's file, and met a team of FBI leaders and military personnel in the old conference room.

Several of the men in the room didn't know anything about the elite, the monitoring department, or the potential risk to society that was ours to protect. The game had changed, and I could tell that this was going to be a very interesting day.

The most dominant presence in the room was General Jim Corbin, though no one ever called him by his first name; most people just addressed him as "sir". General Corbin was tall and burly with a gray buzz-cut and a chiseled face. He wore the experience and scars of battle on his face, the most noticeable of which was the worn eye patch that covered his left eye. His rough military background was evidenced by his demeanor. He had retired from a forty-year military career only to reappear for special government assignments. General Corbin had two other military men with him. They were fully outfitted and looked very important, but they never said a word during the meeting. George and two of his FBI partners were present and dressed in the normal government issued shirt and tie. After George updated the group regarding the elite, the monitoring department and Richard's actions, he asked me to brief the group on Richard's profile. Just like the old days, I instinctively recorded the entire meeting for data filing purposes.

"Richard was categorized as a Class 3 elite which means that he was profiled to have extraordinary strength and endurance." I started to explain. I didn't get far into my description before the questions started coming.

"So, is this guy some sort of superman?" one of George's associates asked.

"No," I replied, "not really. He can't fly and he doesn't have super speed or heat vision. He's definitely not an alien." I paused for a moment hoping to get some reaction to my lame attempt at humor but was only met with stern frowns and confused faces. "Richard's condition stimulates the production of a massive amount of steroids increasing and maintaining his strength far beyond average human ability. His skin reproduction also increases exponentially creating a density in his skin structure that makes it almost impenetrable. His strength and endurance still have limitations, but his limitations are far less than the average person." The FBI agents clearly did not understand everything that I was saying but they were taking notes nonetheless. The military men that accompanied General Corbin never changed facial expressions making it hard to determine if they understood the situation either. They remained stoic throughout the entire briefing.

"So, what exactly are his limitations?" asked General Corbin. His voice was deep and rough, and he spoke with a demeaning tone that clearly conveyed to his listeners that he was the only important person in the room.

"I'm afraid we don't know. Because of the risks involved and the premature death we were seeing in the elite during the early stages of the program, none of them were allowed to develop as an adult to quantify their range. We have never documented a case of a lost or failed restrainer chip."

"Great," said the general, "so we have a superhuman fugitive on our hands, and we don't know how to stop him. Is that what you're saying?" With every word that came from his mouth, the tension mounted even greater in the room. I was expecting him to burst out in anger at any second but tried my best to maintain composure.

"Yes sir", I replied politely, "but we have some options."

"This is an outrage!" the General replied, raising his voice. "The armed forces should have been made aware of this little science experiment years ago! There should have already been protocol in place to handle a situation like this."

"Sir," George interjected, "our proactive approach to identifying and containing any potential threat was very stable. There wasn't a need to escalate any information about the elite further than necessary."

After a brief pause, the General turned his head and fixed his gaze on George.

"Clearly there is now," General Corbin replied sharply. "How many people know about this little operation of yours?" he asked directing his stern expression toward George.

"Some top-level government officials and the agents of this department," George replied. "Everything was kept top secret, and we

71

do have protocol in place to handle upset situations." George's personality couldn't have been more different than General Corbin's. It was interesting to see them banter. General Corbin appeared to be in attack mode while George calmly diffused every argument with his meek and professional responses.

"I want full employment records of everyone who worked here," the General demanded. Taking the lead from George and feeling bold at the moment, I decided to chime in.

"I don't see how that is relevant to tracking down Richard," I interjected. "Everyone that worked here took an oath and signed every type of confidentiality agreement ever printed."

General Corbin's face began taking on a red tint as his harsh glare turned toward me. "This is a matter of national security and…"

"Of course," interrupted George, "all of our records will be made available to you and your men; now, on to the business at hand".

George paused for a moment and then turned toward me in an attempt to regain control of the meeting. "Tom, do you have a plan?"

"Yes sir, I do," I said half smiling. I began to explain our protocol strategy. "When our department was still active, we had protocol outlined for situations like this. The first course of action needs to be civil and diplomatic. We need to try to contact Richard and talk things through. If we can calm him down long enough to explain the situation to him, he may willingly volunteer for a reinsertion of the chip. I think we have enough leverage here to strike a deal with him."

"And if that doesn't work?" asked the General, still irritated at my presence in the room.

"Then we need to look at some more aggressive options," I replied. "Although he is tough and strong, Richard is still normal in other critical body functions. He still needs to breath, eat, drink, and sleep. If we can set a trap for him away from the public and contain him long enough, we can use gas or some other inhibitor on him. Once we get him knocked out, we can keep him incapacitated until a chip can be re-implanted."

"That doesn't sound too hard," General Corbin said. "I think we can handle it from here." The General stood up and his men followed suit. In unison, they started backing away from the conference table as if to leave but stopped abruptly when I interrupted their progress. "With all due respect sir, it's not going to be quite that simple. This is a critical situation, and we need to follow protocol and pursue a negotiable compromise first."

The General immediately gave me a hardened look with his index finger pointed at my face. The vein in his neck bulged as he continued voicing his thoughts. "Listen son, I have lived through more critical situations that you will ever see. I was brought here to bring this guy down, and that's exactly what I am going to do. The last thing I need is some government bird watcher telling me how to do my job."

George immediately spoke up in an attempt to calm the excitement in the room. "Tom," he said, "if it does escalate to more forceful tactics, what are the risks?"

"Well," I continued now directing my communication to George as the only sensible person in the room, "the amount of gas we need to use on Richard may be extremely harmful to innocent bystanders. We need to get him in a contained area by himself."

The General wasn't very pleased by my suggestion but before he could reply, George interjected, "General, we need to work as a team on this. Each of us has an important role to play, and it is paramount that we capture him without a media circus. We can't afford to make the public aware of this program." George always did have a way of diffusing abrasive situations and pulling everyone's focus back on the task at hand. He could sense the friction between the General and me and requested a private session alone with the General after the meeting.

"Gentlemen, we have a very important task at hand here. My hierarchy has requested I personally lead this recovery team to diffuse the situation, and I need each of you to give me your best in order to accomplish our mission," George said as he proceeded to assign tasks to each person. "General Corbin," he said, "we need some riot gear

74

including gas guns and some manpower on this." The General just stared at George, acknowledged his request, but refused to grant him any sign of submission. "Tom, we need your expertise to predict his next move. Since this is all very new to him, he probably isn't very dangerous right now, but it wouldn't take him long to get there if he wanted to be. We must handle this situation with the utmost care."

After a few closing motivational words, George dismissed the team to begin working and requested a reconnect meeting at the end of the day.

General Corbin and George left the conference room to meet in George's office, which gave me a chance to see if the General's companions could speak at all.

"Is he always like that?" I asked one of the soldiers.

"Yes sir," one of the men reluctantly replied as he started gathering some of the papers and files on the table. He wasn't overly excited to talk to me, but clearly he was much more comfortable after General Corbin left the room.

"What happened to his eye?" I asked hoping for more than a two-word answer.

"He was captured during a special operations mission ten years ago in the Middle East," the soldier said. "They tortured his entire team. The General was the only one who survived but not before they gouged his eye out with the end of a bayonet. He was a hero to our country and never got recognized for it".

"How did he escape?" I asked.

"He didn't, the soldier replied. "The two governments came to a diplomatic agreement, and he was released as part of the deal."

I could tell that the two soldiers were not comfortable talking about General Corbin, so I let the conversation end and excused myself to head back to my old office so I could start analyzing some of the file data further. There was a lot to catch up on and not much time to do it.

Tom Marshall Monitor Log File AGAL67

End of Record

Chapter 10

Richard was still on foot and moving north. He was getting into some familiar territory. "The gym," he thought; it was perfect, and it wasn't too far from where he was. Richard quickened his pace as he headed toward the gym. He made it a point to take roads and alleys that weren't very busy so he wouldn't be recognized.

This is crazy, Richard thought to himself as he approached the back door of the gym, *but I don't have a choice here.*

The back door of the gym was always locked from the outside and was labeled as an emergency exit only. Richard knew that the dayshift manager had disabled the emergency exit alarm so he could slip out for extended lunch breaks. Making use of his newfound strength, he forced the door open with his bare hands and slipped inside. He sneaked in unnoticed and started walking down the hall to the locker room. Richard quickly entered the locker room and was about to break into one of the lockers when he heard voices coming closer. He rushed into a bathroom stall and closed the door behind him. He listened and waited. He couldn't tell if the sweat that was running down his face was from the brisk walk to the gym or from nerves. He didn't remember it being there when he got to the gym, but it was unusually hot and humid in the locker room. He breathed a huge sigh of relief when the two men finally left. He slowly walked towards the lockers and pulled the combination lock right off the first one.

Inside the locker was a black and yellow duffel bag. Richard took a quick look over his shoulders and started rummaging through the bag. "Jackpot," Richard whispered to himself finding a wallet, keys, and even a change of clothes. He lifted the shirt up to his chest sizing it up for fit. To his dismay, the clothes were much too large for him. "This guy really needs to be here working out," Richard said to himself quietly as he threw the unwanted items along with the broken lock back in the locker and quickly moved to the next one.

At the second locker he found another wallet, some keys, and a baseball hat. He quickly put the baseball hat on and moved down the row of lockers. After rummaging through six lockers he finally found a decent change of clothes and enough money and car keys to give him plenty of options. Knowing that he had to move quickly, Richard quickly changed out of his torn business attire into the more comfortable workout shirt and sweatpants. He stuffed his old clothes and his newly acquired stolen goods into the duffel bag and quickly left the locker room. As he turned the corner to head down the hall, he heard some footsteps behind him. Richard side-stepped to the water fountain to take a drink. After the man passed by, He bolted for the back door.

Once outside he ran behind the dumpster, opened the duffel bag, and discarded his ripped-up business shirt and pants. He headed toward the front of the building and the packed parking lot. Feeling pressed for time, Richard starting grabbing sets of stolen keys as he walked briskly and began pushing the remote controls to find the right car. When he found a set to a newer or more expensive model, he dropped that set of keys underneath another car. He knew the newer models would have locating devices similar to his own Mercedes.

After the third and fourth attempt, Richard started getting frantic. Finally, the fifth remote was a car that would work. He walked over to the chosen vehicle and after checking over his shoulders one more time he dropped the remaining keys and got inside. After another quick check around the parking lot to see if anyone noticed him, Richard started the car and took off.

"All too easy," Richard said to himself as he left the gym parking lot. He thought he would feel guilty about stealing, but instead it excited him. For all his nervous apprehensions about taking other people's things, Richard felt proud of himself for pulling it off without a single problem. It was freeing to him. Suddenly the rules of society and class that Richard had known all his life seemed a little less rigid. This was an entirely new environment for him, and the experience was like tasting chocolate for the first time.

A few blocks away from the gym, Richard pulled into a small rear alleyway of a strip mall to inventory his stolen goods. Digging to the bottom of the bag he found a pair of socks that appeared clean. He reluctantly verified the socks by giving them a quick smell. "Good enough," he said as he discarded his dress socks and put on the fresh white socks. Unfortunately, Richard didn't have the same luck with the shoes.

"Of course," Richard said to himself as he tried to squeeze his oversized foot into a tennis shoe that just would not fit. Richard hated his business shoes but usually endured the discomfort in the name of fashion. Frustrated with the thought of having to wear his business shoes any longer and being completely mismatched with his attire led him to roll down the passenger side window and throw the tennis shoes out.

Richard began consolidating the cash. He totaled one hundred and thirty-two dollars. *Not bad for ten minutes of work,* he thought as he finished counting the money. Out of the corner of his eye, Richard saw a rear door open from one of the shops in the strip mall and a gangly teenager step out with a full trash bag in his hand. Richard thought fast and reached in the bag again to find a cell phone. He quickly grabbed the phone and placed it up to his ear pretending to talk as the teenage boy walked by, almost touching the front of his car. The boy glanced over at Richard once but then kept walking across the small alleyway toward the dumpster.

Richard kept his eyes on the boy the entire time. After he had glanced over at Richard and then turned his head back toward the dumpster, Richard heard a loud pitched tone followed by a voice in his head. "Weird dude," the voice said. Richard stared at the boy even harder. He hadn't seen the boy move his lips at all, and even if he did, the voice was too clear to be that far away. The speech wasn't clear, but the sound resonated in his head as if he heard it without hearing it. His eyes remain fixed on the boy as he opened the top of the dumpster and threw the bag over all in one swift motion. The boy then started walking back toward the door and looked over at Richard one more time. Richard continued with his imaginary phone conversation but kept his eyes locked on the boy's face. As quickly as he had appeared, the teenager opened the door and disappeared behind it.

"What in the world was that?" Richard said to himself, stuffing the cell phone back into the bag for disposal. "I need to get out of here". Richard started the car and tossed the duffle bag near the dumpster as he passed by.

Anxious to get out of town, Richard opted to abandon his usual trendy salad for lunch and stopped at the nearest fast food restaurant drive-through window.

"Welcome to Burger Barn; can I take your order?" The muffled sound of the speaker was barely understandable. "Yes," Richard said into the speaker raising his voice and slowing his speech. "Give me a number three meal with a mega-size drink and I need an extra French fry with that." Richard's body was craving calories. The overly excited high-pitched voice repeated Richard's order and continued, "That will be seven thirty-eight, please. Drive around to the window." Richard straightened up the pile of clothes in the passenger seat as he drove around to the service window. He didn't want to seem suspicious. As he pulled up to the window, the young girl greeted him with a smile. "Seven thirty-eight please," she said with a bounce in her voice. *Poor girl*, Richard thought to himself, *so young and naïve.* Clearly, she enjoyed her job too much. Richard reached in his pocket retrieving a twenty-dollar bill and handed it to the girl. As he made eye contact with her, he immediately heard a song in his head. It was one of those teenage boy band pop songs that was extremely catchy but didn't make any sense. He didn't know the name of the song but remembered hearing it in a store somewhere. The sharp pain in his head returned making him wince slightly. As he handed her the money, he noticed that her head bopped ever so slightly to the beat of the song that had now consumed every conscious brain cell in his head.

"Here is your change and your meal sir," the girl said as she handed Richard his food with a beaming smile still on her face. "Thank you," Richard replied, now more motivated than ever to get away from the Burger Barn. Richard set the bag down in the passenger seat and made a failed attempt to fit the mega-size drink in the vehicle's tiny cup holder as he slowly pulled forward away from the service window.

Suddenly out of the corner of his eye, Richard saw a little boy darting in front of his car from a parked vehicle across from the restaurant. Richard slammed on the brakes bringing the coasting vehicle to a complete stop. In a reflex action, he also tightened his grip on the steering wheel with his left hand while his right hand crushed his mega-size cup gushing soda all over his newly acquired pants. The little boy's mother shot out of the same vehicle and chased her son into the restaurant yelling the entire way. Just as she entered the restaurant, the ice-cold soda soaked its way through Richard's pants. With a grunt of frustration, Richard punched the dashboard of the car breaking the plastic and rendering the radio useless. "Come on!" Richard sternly said to himself, now feeling like the entire world was out to get him.

Richard salvaged what was left of his drink and practically inhaled his meal as he pulled out on the main street headed toward the interstate. Just as he was finishing the last bite of his greasy burger, Richard spotted a dilapidated department store sign up ahead. The thought of entering one of those low-class bargain chain department stores was uncomfortable for Richard. He was much more comfortable shopping in upper class specialty stores, but he was desperate for a pair of dry pants and some comfortable shoes. He drove into the parking lot and waiting for an opportune moment when the number of people around seemed to be diminished.

Richard knew that he couldn't stay in one place too long, so he quickly got out of his recently acquired car and walked with a fast pace to the front door of the store. After entering, he paused for a moment to get his bearings and began searching for the "Men's Clothing" section. To his dismay, the men's clothes were all the way in the back corner of the store allowing many fellow shoppers the opportunity to stare and snicker at his miss-matched soda stained attire. Richard wasted no time grabbing a pack of boxer shorts and a pair of jeans before heading to the shoe section of the store. With every stranger's glance, Richard felt more embarrassed and more hurried to get out of the store. He grabbed the first pair of tennis shoes that he thought looked halfway decent and sat down to try them on. To his surprise, the first pair that he picked fit fine. Richard threw them back in the box, put his dress shoes back on and made his way to the front of the store.

Not wanting to waste any time, Richard sought out the express line register. The store had thirty-two checkout lines, but only four of them were staffed and people were lined up at each one. He walked up to the end of the line behind an older man holding his prescription medicine and a box of cookies. Ahead of them was an older black lady who clearly had more than ten items in her cart. The pace at which she unloaded her cart revealed that she did not understand the meaning of "express lane." Richard kept quiet so that he wouldn't attract unnecessary attention, but he was visibly irritated with having to wait. After what seemed like hours, the old lady finally placed the last bag of merchandise in her cart and moved on.

The old man shuffled forward as the cashier scanned his items. She was a very large black lady who appeared to be a newly trained cashier and was completely unfamiliar with the register. She gave the old man his total and his shaky, wrinkled hand reached in his pocket and pulled out a checkbook. The old man then began to write out his check slowly and cautiously. Still trying to contain himself, Richard let out an audible sigh. The cashier looked straight at Richard for just a few seconds. Her lips didn't move, but her eyes glared right into his eyes. As plainly as if she had yelled it out loud, Richard heard her thought. *"Boy, you better chill out and wait your turn."* She then glanced down at his pants as her voice again filled Richard's head. *"Don't know what you in such a hurry for anyway, looks like you already peed your pants."*

Just then, Richard winced as a sharp pain permeated the right side of his head. He quickly closed his eyes as the pain hit like a knife and slowly diminished. He had a few seconds to compose himself as the elderly man in front of him finished writing his check and handed it to the cashier. She processed his check and handed him the receipt as Richard moved forward with his merchandise. He had a bewildered look on his face as he began to realize what was happening. Richard attempted to test his theory by staring at her face while she scanned each of his items. He heard nothing until she had finished scanning and bagging his items. She looked up at his eyes and said, "Fifty-three twenty-two."

Richard stared at her trying to listen to her thoughts but heard nothing. A few short moments after the scene had become painfully awkward, Richard broke the silence by saying, "Oh, okay," and immediately fumbled for the wad of cash in his pocket. Slightly embarrassed by the situation, he quickly finished his purchase transaction and walked briskly out of the store.

Richard moved his car to a more secluded area behind the store building to change from his stained apparel to his stiff new boxers, pants, and shoes. After one quick stop to drop another forty-five dollars in gasoline, Richard drove toward Interstate 85 northbound in a desperate quest for help. He knew he had to get more money along the way, but he had already spent too much time in Atlanta and started to get paranoid at every police car he saw. There would be more opportunities along the way to stock up on cash and supplies. The important thing for Richard now was getting to Jennifer.

Chapter 11

Tom Marshall Monitor Log Personal File AJMS46

I didn't have much time for research after my first encounter with the team, so I did as much as I could and started early the very next morning. I had documented Richard enough to know that he was uncomfortable at the thought of losing his affluent life. He wasn't about to give up all that he had worked for in exchange for a prison suit and a caged room. I spent a lot of time analyzing Richard and his behavior patterns. I knew that he liked to keep his wallet stocked with cash and that being void of all resources would drive him insane. He was smart enough not to go back to his house; he knew they would be waiting for him there. He knew that he couldn't call on his parents for help; the police would have gotten to them first. Still, Richard wasn't going to deal with this on his own. He would be looking for help from someone he trusted.

As I continued to piece together the data that we had, George walked into my office. "Do you have a minute to talk?" George asked as he took a seat in the chair across from my desk.

"Sure," I replied, intrigued to hear what he had to say. "Tom, I really appreciate your willingness to jump right back in and help us out; after the way everything went down, I wasn't sure how you would react. Honestly, I didn't think you would come back to help".

I was stunned; surely George knew me better than that. I gave my whole life to this job; I was made for this. I was surprised he couldn't tell how excited I was about being back in the game, but he was right about one thing- the way everything went down was wrong, and I hadn't gotten over it.

"Well George, I hate to say I told you so, but I think I recall mentioning that it was going to be a mistake to close down our department." I said with a grin.

George chuckled, "Yeah I am quite sure you mentioned it once or twice. If it means anything at all, Tom, my hands were tied. There was nothing I could have done. When this situation with Richard hit and my leadership asked who we should call, I knew there was only one guy who could help us out of this mess. You are the best of the best and I am glad to have you back."

"Thanks George," I replied. "That really does mean a lot." George stood up and turned toward the door.

"Just let me know what you need Tom. We're going to take better care of you this time around," he said as he walked out of the office.

Although he had just turned sixty-one years old, George didn't look a day over fifty. He had been good to the department and to me. We all had a lot of respect for him. He was the one that fought for me to take on more when others were a little reluctant to let one monitor take on so much. George had confided in me about the discovery of the elite and some of the early days of monitoring. He was a good leader who always took the time to slip in words of encouragement for those who were under him. He knew the sacrifices that his team made and took every chance he had to remind them that he was grateful. Today was no exception.

I had forgotten how much George had done for me. After the layoff a few months ago, I was angry with him for not fighting harder for the department. There was a hint of guilt as I watched him leave my office. Of course George fought for the department and fought for me; it was in his nature to do so.

George was a fighter. He was a man who fought for his marriage and family when his job demanded so much time. George had a beautiful wife and three great kids. He had been happily married for 37 years, but there was a time when George admitted to me that his life at home wasn't as happy as it seemed. I remember the day when George walked in my office with a serious look on his face as if he had just woken up from a bad dream. "Tom, I know you are used to meeting up with me every week for an update, but don't expect a meeting or a call for a couple of weeks," he said as he stood in the doorway of my office, not wanting to sit down. I could tell that his focus was somewhere else and that he was anxious to leave.

"What's wrong George?" I asked.

"I am not proud of this, Tom, but I have been working so hard that my marriage isn't doing so hot right now. Danielle threatened to leave me, and I can't let her do that. She means too much to me. I just couldn't see it until now."

"You are a good man, George. I wouldn't expect anything less," I replied, trying to be as encouraging to him as he had been to all of us for the past several years. After that day, George took some vacation time he had accumulated and dedicated time to his wife Danielle and their kids. He never said anything more to me about the issue, but whatever he did worked. From that time on, George was able to save his marriage and balance his family life with the ever-increasing demands of the job. He stopped traveling for work so much and was religious about leaving every day at five o'clock, even if it meant taking some work home with him.

George and Danielle had weekly lunch dates set up and spoke to each other throughout the day on the phone like they were young teenagers who had just fallen in love. His office board was covered in family pictures, and he would always take a few with him when he did have a business trip. George only traveled twice a year on business and never provided us with any details regarding his itinerary. I consistently asked him what these mystery trips were all about, but he always just gave me that charming grin and said, "Top secret, Tom, top secret". It bothered me a little to be left out of the loop after I had worked so hard for maximum government security access. George knew my irritation and playfully taunted me with it every chance he got. Most of the time he would try his best British accent and say, "I'm off to England, Thomas." It truly was a pathetic accent, and I knew he didn't even have a passport. I would banter back that these semi-annual rendezvous trips were a clever disguise to hide his secret girlfriend in a far-away land, but the reality is that I knew he was loyal to Danielle. Every time I asked him about Danielle and the kids, his face lit up and he would talk endlessly about how proud he was of his children.

There was a part of me that was jealous of George. He had so much that I wanted. He was part of the original monitoring group. He was part of the team that compiled all of the data analysis on the first elite. He had earned respect and honor - all while balancing his life and saving his marriage. Whenever I heard George tell me about one of his vacations or something that one of his children accomplished, I sometimes wished that I could tell him about my life outside of work, but there wasn't anything to tell.

Shortly after George walked out of my office, the latest police report notifications started coming in on my computer. George had already requested that we get copied on every emergency or law enforcement call in the area. I scanned through the usual domestic disturbance and automobile accident headers to come across one that grabbed my attention. It was a recently filed burglary incident at the Hard Core Gym. I immediately opened the details of the report and started reading to myself.

"Hard Core Gym...forced entry through the rear door...several lockers in the men's locker room...locks broken off...car keys, clothes, money reported missing...one automobile theft." The more I read, the more I was convinced that this was Richard's handiwork. The Hard Core Gym wasn't on the best side of town, but it was on the way home from work for Richard. He was a loyal member of the gym, visiting consistently every time he was in town.

Richard wasn't a thief by nature, but he had a strong enough personality to do what he needed to do to survive. According to the police report, a blunt tool was used to force the rear door open and some surveillance video was captured. "Video footage would definitely be worth looking at," I said to myself as the excitement of feeling valued began to swell. The police station wasn't far from my office, so I decided to chase down the video footage.

"George, come with me for a minute, I think I have a lead," I said popping my head in George's office. "I am going to need your FBI clearance to pull some information at the police station."

"What about General Corbin?" George asked as he grabbed his keys from the desk drawer and began to follow me out.

"No time for a debriefing on this," I replied, "we need to move fast." Of course I was intentionally leaving the General out of this for now. *Let's see how forty years of military bullying stacks up to true detective skills,"* I said in my head.

"We'll be right back," George said, passing General Corbin in the hall and walking briskly to keep up with me. I flew out the front door with George close behind. "Slow down, Tom; I'm not as young as I used to be," he said.

I got to my car and started the engine before George made it to the passenger side door. "What do you have, Tom?" he said as he got in and closed the door.

"There was a burglary report at the Hard Core Gym," I replied. "We need to see about getting our hands on the surveillance video. Do you think you can help with that?"

"Sure," George said. "That reminds me; I need to get your government access reinstated. I'll start working on that tomorrow. Tell me more about what you think Richard is doing."

"Richard has always been resource dependent. He's looking to get some base level of survival resources, and he'll be looking to get some help. The items stolen at the gym represent the basic necessities for

Richard: money, clothes, and transportation. He has a membership there and knows the layout well."

"Great," George responded. "Once we get a visual identification, we can get the team back together and talk next steps."

"George, we can do this without having the military goons involved. I know Richard's personality and profile. I can track him down and..."

"And what?" George interrupted, "how do you plan on stopping him Tom? Listen, you are my number one guy, and I am grateful to have you working on this with me, but we need to make sure we can contain Richard before things get too far out of control. I have been given some leeway here, but I'm not calling all the shots on this one. Quite frankly, we're stuck with the team we have, and I'm afraid we might end up needing them."

We drove up to the police station as George was finishing his mini lecture. I didn't agree with him on this, but it wasn't the time or place for an argument.

George worked quickly to get us access to the video footage at Hard Core Gym. The picture quality was terrible, but it was Richard. George immediately escalated the auto theft classification and notified all of the local authorities in the surrounding areas.

As I suspected, the gym was just the beginning. Clearly, he was on the move. We just didn't know where he was going. Richard's crime spree was nothing short of pitiful. He only struck two small convenient stores, which made it exceedingly difficult for us to separate him from some of the other small-time criminals so that we could track his path. I hoped that he was smart enough to stick with the smaller thefts out of necessity, but I was worried that Richard was far more driven than that. The love of power and money breeds more lust for the same. I knew that as he became more comfortable with his newly discovered abilities, he would get bolder in his felonies. After reviewing the maps and the crimes that we could link him to, I became convinced that he was definitely headed toward the northwest part of the country. I was sure he was being driven by a deeper desperation, but I didn't know what it was.

Reluctantly, I shared the information that I had with the team in one of the follow up meetings that George scheduled daily.

"We've linked Richard to several small theft events north of Atlanta and along Interstate 81. It appears that he is heading north. Richard graduated from the University of Pennsylvania and may be returning to Philadelphia to look for some help. So far, he hasn't done anything unusual enough to attract the attention of the media, but he is getting more brazen as he becomes more comfortable with his abilities. My recommendation is that we move the team to Philadelphia and plan a capture strategy from there."

"Excellent work, Tom," George replied. "Grab all the files and data you need. I'll arrange for a jet to pick us up at the airport. The sooner we get there and make contact, the better."

Much to my satisfaction, General Corbin stayed silent for this debriefing, but I could still sense an environment of disgust in the way we were handling this scenario. I was leery of the General's overall approach to this. He seemed to want to treat this like hunting a wild animal. Although I was excited to be back in the action, this wasn't a hunt at all for me. This was Richard. This was the guy that I watched grow up. I needed to find a way to deal with the situation without the General imposing control and messing this up.

Tom Marshall Monitor Log Personal File AJMS46
End of Record

Chapter 12

Jennifer Stokes grew up in a small town outside of Charlotte, North Carolina. Her father was a blue-collar worker for the local power company, and her mother worked part time as a substitute teacher for the public school system. Jenny was the oldest of three children and voted most likely to succeed by her high school graduating class. She was a brilliant young lady but a bit on the shy side and not much for social interaction. Jenny's passion in life was to help people. She was fascinated with medical journals and the latest scientific research on the functions of the human body. Jenny's constant research and hard work yielded her a full scholarship to the University of Pennsylvania's medical program, a blessing that her low-income parents were extremely grateful for.

It was late at night, and Jenny was sound asleep when she heard the desperate knocking at her door. Her eyes opened, but she remained still for a moment. She sat up slowly and listened again to make sure she wasn't just dreaming. Suddenly, the knock returned louder and faster than the first time. She threw the covers back, jumped out of bed and grabbed her robe. She was still tying the fabric belt of her robe around her waist as she stumbled through the living room of her small apartment when she reached the door. She turned on the outside light and peered through the peephole in the door. Jenny gasped slightly at the sight of Richard and then quickly fumbled to get the door unlocked. Briefly, she thought about running back to the bathroom to at least brush her hair, but the shock of the situation coupled with Richard's rough appearance quickly brought her back to the reality that something was very wrong.

"Richard, what are you doing here? What's wrong?" Jenny asked in a groggy voice. She was never one to keep up with the news and was oblivious to the events in Richards's life the past few days.

"Jenny," Richard said as he quickly moved into the apartment living room not waiting for an invitation, "I'm in a lot of trouble, and I need your help."

"Why? What's going on Richard? You're really freaking me out."

"I just need a place to stay for a couple of days. I need to see a doctor, but it has to be someone we can trust. Something has changed about me, and I can't figure it out."

Richard was clearly exhausted and not making much sense, but Jenny was still smitten enough with him to be compassionate. Staying true to her personality, Jennifer took him in and set him up on the couch to rest for the night. Richard was still shaken. The adrenaline rush and the anxiety of being a wanted man fueled his body. Although he made several attempts at communicating with Jennifer, he kept stopping short. There wasn't an easy way to explain everything that had happened to him.

As he sat on the couch, he felt somewhat at ease for the first time in days. He didn't have to worry about where he was getting his next meal or where he could close his eyes and rest or if someone was going to recognize him and report him to the police. The comfort and security he felt at Jennifer's place dropped his adrenaline level, and his body immediately felt weak and lethargic.

"I'm sorry, Jen. I just need to…" Richard said slowly as his face began to fall and his eyelids grew heavy.

"Richard, just lie down and rest." Jennifer said in a very motherly tone, walking toward the old brown couch with a spare blanket. "We can figure all this out in the morning."

Richard fell asleep quickly on Jennifer's old couch. It was worn but soft and gave him a much-needed sense of comfort. Jennifer was still quite perplexed by his visit, but she was glad to see him despite the unusual circumstances. She walked back to the front door, locked it and then turned out the front light. As she passed by the couch, she stopped for a minute to watch him sleep before walking back to her own bedroom to get some rest.

The daylight appeared through the front window of Jennifer's apartment and hit Richard directly in the face as he slowly woke up from his short rest. His eyes were still heavy, and the scent of scrambled eggs filled the modest single-bedroom apartment. Richard raised his head and then sat up slowly rubbing his eyes.

"Good morning, Sunshine," Jennifer said as she approached him with a full plate and glass of orange juice. "Hard scrambled, right?" Always modest, Jennifer had pink long pajamas that looked like they belonged to a full grown eight-year-old girl. Her pajamas were covered by a dark pink fuzzy robe and complete with pink slippers.

"Um...yes" Richard replied still trying to wake up. "Smells great, Jenny, thanks."

"You weren't making much sense last night Richard. What's going on?" Jenny said as she took a seat beside him on the couch.

Richard sat silent for a moment not knowing where to start. He placed his elbows on his knees and folded his hands. He bent his head down slightly searching for the right words to say. "Did you see the plane crash on the news a few weeks ago?"

"Yes," Jenny replied. "It made all the headlines."

"I was on that plane", Richard said immediately invoking a concerned look on Jenny's face.

"Oh my...are you okay, Richard?" Jenny asked as she moved her hand to his back and started to gently rub it.

"Ever since that accident, there's been something different. My muscles are swollen; I am stronger and faster than I have ever...than anyone has ever been."

"Richard, I don't understand. Maybe you need to lie back down for a while."

"No, Jenny, listen to me," Richard said frustrated that she wasn't getting what he was talking about. "There's something else, too. When I look at someone's eyes, sometimes I can hear what they're thinking."

"What?" Jenny said now a bit puzzled. She turned sideways on the couch and leaned back against the arm of the sofa.

"It's hard to believe, I know, but it's true," Richard replied. "It gives me such a headache. The pain is terrible. I need to get some medicine for the pain...I need someone to help me figure out what's going on."

"Richard, you have to understand that this isn't making much sense to me. I haven't seen you in months, and then you show up in the middle of the night at my front door and tell me that you can read people's minds. I just don't know what to do with that."

"Look at me Jenny; I can prove it to you," Richard said as he turned sideways to look at Jenny's eyes.

Jenny hesitated at first. She stared down at her own feet for a moment. She believed him enough to be reluctant to let him look into her eyes. The thought scared her. She sat silent for a minute while Richard continued to look at her face longing for the eye contact that would prove his point. After a moment, she decided to humor Richard and looked up at his eyes.

"Now," Richard said, "think about something that I wouldn't possibly know about you."

She tried hard to fight her own thoughts. If he were telling the truth, then she would be vulnerable. In the end, she couldn't hold it back any longer. She looked intently into his eyes and as much as she tried to hold back, she instinctively thought of the one expression that she had never been able to say to Richard. *I love you.*

Richard's eyes got big, and he pulled away from her with a shocked look on his face. His eyes were locked on to hers for a few seconds longer before the pain consumed him. He winced and bent over bringing his head down almost to his knees. He covered his eyes with his hands while letting out a grunt that broke the awkward silence of the moment.

Now she knew that he was telling the truth. Now he knew the secret that she had hidden so well. Jenny's faced turned red in embarrassment. She quickly stood up and started fumbling for an excuse to leave the room. Richard just sat there still stunned. His hands covered his tightly shut eyes as he tried to recover from the sharp pain in his head. Without a good reason to excuse herself from the room and realizing that it was all too late to take the thought back or try to explain it away, Jennifer sat back down on the couch and turned toward Richard sheepishly.

"Richard, I..." She started to say before being interrupted by the motion of Richard's hand. With his eyes still closed, Richard

102

moved his hand out motioning her to wait until the pain subsided. The moment was awkward and seemed to drag on for hours.

After a minute of silence, Richard let out a breath, lowered his hands and opened his eyes. His gaze was downward toward the floor. The pain was still evident on his face, though it had subsided quite a bit. "I need help, Jenny. I don't know where to go." Both of them did their best to ignore the awkward feeling and move back to the original conversation.

"You may be in luck," Jenny said still trying to regain her composure. "A lot of my medical research friends will be with me at Camp Pennington. You can go with me. I am sure they wouldn't mind seeing if there was anything they can do to help."

"Camp Pennington?"

"Yes, I was supposed to meet my friend Ashley there tonight. The kids are scheduled to arrive tomorrow morning. If we leave soon, we can still make it in time."

"I don't think I am up for camping," Richard replied.

"It's not that type of camp. Camp Pennington is for children who are terminally ill. Several of the leading medical researchers and doctors will be there. This is one of the very few events these kids have in their life that is remotely normal. It will be good for you to get away for a few days to sort out your thoughts and maybe get some help with your headaches."

Jennifer's tone and choice of words solidified the plan without giving Richard much of a chance to decline. "We need to get you some clothes and supplies so we can start packing."

"Listen Jenny, I don't want a lot of people to know about this," Richard said concerned about drawing too much attention to himself. He didn't want to risk someone making some correlations between his abilities and the recent newscasts.

Jennifer, though still embarrassed by the whole situation, felt some level of relief in knowing that Richard read her thought. It was freeing to her, and she never even had to say it. She knew that the only thing she could do now was forge on ahead and try to help him where she could. This would be unchartered territory for their otherwise platonic relationship. It was both frightening and exciting for her. Richard was at her mercy, and it gave her a chance to pull him into her world – a place he had never shown much interest in going before.

"The kids are really great," Jenny continued as she got up and started cleaning up after breakfast. "Ashley works at the children's hospital in Atlanta. Her son Joshua always comes with her; you'll really like them. Last year was my first year volunteering, but Ashley has been a big part of the camp for years."

Richard remained silent, still trying to analyze the situation even though the decision to go had already been made for him. Jennifer had finished taking the dishes into the kitchen and passed by Richard once more on her way to the bedroom. "Now come on sleepyhead, we need to go shopping before we hit the road."

Chapter 13

The five-and-a-half-hour ride in Jennifer's little Honda was grueling after being in a car the entire previous day, but Richard was at her disposal. Jennifer had her little car loaded up with toys, clothes, and games for the kids in addition to her own two suitcases and one for Richard's new wardrobe. The trip helped Richard get his mind off the current circumstances. Although he still felt no attraction to Jennifer, it was nice being in the company of someone familiar who was sincere about helping him. After the first few hours of hearing Jennifer talk about the camp, the kids, her friend Ashley, and her passion for helping to find a cure for some of the illnesses these kids had, Richard finally opened up about all the things that happened to him.

There were a few moments in the journey that Jennifer was more than a bit frightened to hear how Richard accidentally killed a highway patrol officer and how he had run from the police. Of course, Richard put a positive spin on the story as much as he could and made himself out to be the victim in all of the events. Jennifer managed to ignore the voice inside of her that was prodding her to get far away from Richard and move on with her own life. She had already made herself vulnerable and desperately longed for something more to develop with Richard despite the circumstances.

It was already dark when they reached the remote camp amidst the mountains. Jennifer had almost missed the weathered sign that pointed off the main road toward the entrance of the camp. They traveled a winding dirt road that led them between two very tall mountain cliffs. The scene looked menacing at night.

"Are you sure you know where you are going?" Richard asked.

"I was hoping to get here before dark so it would be easier to find, but SOMEONE changed those plans. And yes, I'm sure. There is only one road in and out of the camp sight, and we're on it." Jennifer replied as they finally reached the front gate of the camp.

Richard thought that the place was somewhat primitive and poorly lit. His experience with summer camp was more of an upper-class affair and generally took place at the local county club resort. She finally stopped in a grassy clearing that doubled as a parking lot. There were about thirty cars in the field all parked in crooked rows. Jen parked next to a blue Honda closer to the road. The entrance of the camp was to their right past the cars. There were two wooden buildings with dirty glass windows and a wide path separating them. A dim light was on inside the building on the right and just as they pulled up, a silhouette appeared in the window for a minute and then dashed toward the front door.

"Jenny! You finally made it," the woman said in a screaming whisper as she briskly approached Jennifer's car. Jennifer quickly got out of the car and trotted over to the woman, giving her a warm hug.

"Hey, Ashley, sorry I'm late. I had a delay getting started this morning. It is so good to see you."

"And who is this?" Ashley asked as Richard stepped out of the car and started to stretch.

"This is my friend Richard," Jennifer replied.

"Oh, is this THE Richard?" Ashley remarked with a grin on her face.

Jenny's eyes got big and locked onto Ashley face as if she were silently screaming for her to keep her mouth closed.

"Jen, you know that Mr. Pennington is going to want to make sure we have a background check on your friend, right?"

"Ashley, he's fine, really," Jennifer said wanting so badly to convince Ashley and to convince herself that Richard needed to stay with her. "I'll vouch for him. He'll be a great help this week with the kids. You know we always need more men around to help; some of these kids don't have a father figure."

It was a bit dirty, but Jennifer knew that statement would strike a chord with Ashley. Her son, Joshua, was fifteen years old and never knew his own father. Ashley had gotten pregnant at seventeen years old. Her committed boyfriend assured her that he would stay with her and take care of her, but after a few

109

months, the reality of the situation was too much for him to handle. Quickly and cowardly, he left. Ashley's parents helped her through the pregnancy and helped her raise Joshua, but they were never happy about the situation. Still, Ashley worked hard and earned her nursing degree with a combination of night school and online courses. She was one of the best nurses at the children's hospital, and she was instrumental in setting up and running Camp Pennington.

"It's really nice to meet you Ashley," Richard interjected while he held out his arm ready to shake her hand. "Jenny has told me so much about you."

Ashley gingerly shook his hand. "Ok, listen, it's already late and we've got almost two hundred kids that are going to show up in the morning, not to mention Mr. Pennington will be here first thing. We need to get some rest. Richard, the male camp counselor's cabin is over there," she said pointing to the rustic log cabin off to the left. "Jen, let me help you with your stuff so you can get some sleep. Big day tomorrow."

Both Richard and Jennifer grabbed their suitcases and parted ways heading to their own cabins. Richard sensed that Ashley didn't like him, but he wasn't overly concerned. He knew that Jennifer would stay true to her word, and he was confident that his own charm would soon win her over.

Richard made the short hike to a dilapidated wood building, tripping twice over tree roots and sticks in the way. Unsure of what to do, he slowly opened the front door. The door had two screen panels and a knob that desperately needed replacing. At the halfway point, the door creaked, and the musty smell of aged pine stopped Richard in his tracks.

"Hey," a groggy voice said in the darkness.

"Hi, my name is Richard. I'm Jenny's friend."

"Oh, hey, Richard. I'm Greg. We weren't expecting you, but it's good to have you on board. There's an empty cot to your left by the window," the voice whispered as a shadowy figure approached from the darkness.

Richard couldn't make out any distinctive facial features in the darkness, but Greg sounded nice enough to trust. There were six cots laid out in the small room: three perpendicular to the wall on the right and three to the wall on the left. The one near the window that Greg mentioned was easier to see as the dim moonlight penetrated the room. Greg continued to approach until he got within handshaking distance and extended his arm toward Richard.

"Nice to meet you," Greg said still half asleep. "The bathroom is straight back if you need it, and there are spare blankets at the bottom of the nightstand near your cot. You can meet the rest of the guys in the morning."

"Thanks, Greg."

Richard made his way toward the window while Greg flopped back down on his cot in the back and immediately started snoring.

The musty smell had become familiar in his nose and didn't bother him as much anymore. Richard kicked off his shoes and slumped down in the cot for another short night of sleep.

It seemed as though only seconds had passed when Richard was jolted awake by the sound of movement in the room. His eyes opened wide, but his body felt like a giant sack of potatoes. He really needed a good eight hours on a mattress more than three inches thick, but that wasn't going to happen anytime soon. He reached up to rub his eyes and caught the attention of a familiar voice.

"Good morning. "

The sun was just breaking over the horizon providing enough light for Richard to see the room and its occupants more, but it was still early. It was obvious that Greg had been awake for a while. His early morning greeting was much livelier than the short discussion they had when Richard first walked in.

"Sorry to wake you so early, but there's a lot to do before the kids get here," Greg said as he stood at the end of Richard's cot. Richard partially sat up, still trying to muster up some energy in the rest of his body. The cabin didn't look much better in the light than it did in the dark. The scuffed floor, walls, and ceiling were all made of wood and appeared as if it was built well over fifty years ago. The rafters held generations of dust and spider webs. There were two small windows on each of the side walls and one door on the back wall that led to the shared bathroom. As Richard perused the room with his eyes, he noticed that there were two other guys in the cabin that he did not recognize. One was brushing his teeth in the bathroom while the other was rummaging through a large green duffle bag that doubled as a suitcase.

"That's Chad, and Ron's the guy with the white teeth," Greg said. Chad turned his head to make eye contact while Ron just waved from the doorway of the bathroom. All three of the guys looked to be in their early twenties. As he sat up on his cot, Richard noticed that the bed in the far corner was still lumpy, but he couldn't imagine anyone sleeping through the noise that the other guys were making.

"What time is it?" he asked.

"Seven fifteen," Greg answered as he walked toward the lumpy cot in the corner. "Mr. Pennington will be here at nine, and the kids show up at ten."

"How many kids again?" Richard asked still a bit groggy.

"One hundred seventy-three. And you, my friend, are now one of the elite group of only fifteen male chaperones within a one hundred mile radius. Most of the rest of the guys are sleeping in the boys cabins just over there," Greg said as he pointed his finger toward the window over Richard's cot.

Greg made his way over to the lumpy cot which, upon further examination, contained a covered body. One little foot stuck out of the blanket at the side of the bed.

"Get up, Little J," Greg said giving the cot a quick jolt. "And this little sleep monster is Joshua, our camp mascot and the youngest member of our little boy band." A grunt could be heard from the still motionless lump under the blanket.

"We would make a terrible band," Chad said as he made his way to the front door. "Let's go, gents. We have a prep meeting at seven-thirty." Ron followed shortly after, and Joshua finally emerged from under the blanket and made his way to the bathroom as Greg started straightening up the room.

Richard, who was accustomed to taking a shower in the morning, sat on the edge of his cot waiting for his turn in the bathroom. Within a few minutes Joshua emerged and joined Greg as they headed for the door.

"We're meeting by the lake in ten minutes. Don't be late."

"Any chance there will be coffee at this meeting?" Richard asked as he walked toward the bathroom door.

"No," Greg said with a smile on his face, "but once you get a fresh breath of nature, you'll be awake enough."

"Somehow, I doubt that."

Chapter 14

Freshly showered and feeling more awake, Richard strolled down the small hillside behind the cabin toward the lake. The camp didn't look quite as menacing during the day. The landscape was filled with trees and small patches of open pastures. It was set in a valley surrounded by mountains. To his right he saw a series of trails leading to different sections of the camp. One trail led to a large building with vent pipes protruding from the roof and a diesel generator adjacent to it. Richard assumed this was the mess hall. Another building with a large red cross painted on the side was so close to the mess hall that it almost touched it. The widest trail led up a small hill where a cluster of fifteen cabins were built side by side forming a semicircle with a large fire pit in the center. To his left, another wide trail extended up a steeper hill and disappeared in a thicket of trees. Directly in front on him, he saw the lake where a large group of people all wearing the same color shirts were gathered.

Richard knew that he was late for the preparation meeting, so he tried to approach quietly and unnoticed. He scanned the group not wanting to look at any one person long enough for fear that his headaches would return. His entrance did not escape the sight of Jenny. She gave him a look of reprimand similar to the one his mother used to give him when he was young. As soon as she caught his eye, he glanced away and pretended not to see her scowl. Greg, who was clearly one of the main leaders, was addressing the group with some final instructions for the day. Richard was able to catch the last part of his speech.

"...so any final questions?" Greg asked. Richard had a lot of questions, but he stayed quiet since he missed most of the meeting. "Ok, so to recap – Mr. Pennington will be here in about an hour, and the kids will start arriving at ten. You must have your nametags on. Everyone helps getting the kids checked in and to their cabins. If your name is on a cabin, you own it, and you're responsible for the kids in your cabin," Greg said and then turned to Richard. "If your name is not on a cabin, you stay in the counselor's cabins at the entrance to the camp. Alright everyone, please find your cabins and your nametags. Meet back here at nine o'clock. Mr. Pennington is going to want to talk to all of us."

The crowd started to disperse. Everyone seemed to know what to do and where to go. Everyone but Richard. Jenny trotted up to him, grabbed him by the arm just above the elbow, and walked briskly with him. She pulled him away from the crowd as casually as possible and started scolding him in a whispering voice. "Being late to the prep meeting is not a great way to make a first impression."

"Listen Jen, I'm sorry. I've been through a lot the past few days and…"

"You're right," Jenny interrupted. "I know." Her tone quickly faded from agitated to sympathetic. "I just want you to blend in and be accepted here. I need to go talk to Greg. He probably doesn't know you're not a registered counselor, and he needs to hear that from me before Ashley lets the cat out of the bag and freaks everyone out. For now, you need to go back to the cabin you stayed in last night and hang out until Mr. Pennington gets here."

It seemed like only a minute or two before Greg came through the rickety front door of the cabin. With only cots for furniture, Greg sat down on the bed across from Richard.

"So, Jenny tells me that you are looking for some help with headaches?" Greg asked.

"Yes," Richard replied wondering how much Jenny told him. Without wanting to, Richard looked up at Greg's eyes and immediately, the sharp pain returned. Richard heard Greg's next sentence before it was spoken, but the words were cut short by Richard's apparent pain.

"Wow", Greg said in a quieter voice, "that looks like it hurts. Listen, why don't you lay here for a bit and rest up. I'll check up on you when Mr. Pennington arrives."

Richard didn't verbally respond but complied with the suggestion. He slowly laid his head down on the flat pillow and closed his eyes still winching from the pain. For the next few moments, all Richard could hear was the rustling of the trees and some voices off in the distance behind the cabin. He felt himself dozing off for a few minutes but then opened his eyes wide to keep himself from falling asleep. Every passing minute was a battle against his body to stay awake, and then he gave in to the exhaustion and fell asleep. The next sound Richard heard was a knocking on the cabin door.

"Richard," the feminine voice called, "Richard, are you okay?"

"Jenny? Yes…fine…I guess I dozed off."

"Hurry up. Mr. Pennington is almost here."

Richard felt as though he had slept for hours. His body was still heavy, but he got up and walked briskly to the bathroom to check his hair and make a few corrections. He then joined Jenny who was standing outside next to the front door.

As he left the cabin, Jenny quickly came to his side, and they walked to the grassy parking area together. Several of the other camp counselors and helpers gathered around though the crowd was not as large as it was at the lake.

A black car pulled up into the grassy area at the front of the camp, and from the rear door an older gentleman appeared. He looked as though he was in his mid-sixties. The way everyone talked about him in such high esteem, Richard expected to see a man in a business suit, but he emerged from the car in a pair of jeans and a blue button-down shirt. With his upbringing, Richard immediately recognized that this was still designer attire. The old man had a semicircle of white hair around his bald head and bright blue eyes.

Several of the camp counselors walked up to greet him, but Jenny stood still next to Richard as though she was waiting for her turn to talk to Mr. Pennington.

After a few minutes, Jenny caught Mr. Pennington's eye and he walked toward them.

"Good morning, Mr. Pennington," Jenny said with a smile. "This is my friend Richard. He wanted to join me this week to help out with the kids."

"Theodore Pennington," he said extending his hand. "You can call me Ted. It's nice to meet you." Richard noticed that no one called him by his first name, but it seemed to stem from respect rather than fear.

"Richard..." he hesitated just for a second as the voice in his head told him not to use his real last name. "Richard Alexander. It's nice to meet you, too," he responded and gave Mr. Pennington a firm handshake.

"We're always happy to have some extra help around here, Richard. Let's sit down and talk for a minute after I meet with everyone. Jenny, it's a joy to see you again. Thank you both for coming."

With a warm smile, Mr. Pennington turned his attention to Greg who escorted him toward the lake. As they walked, Mr.

Pennington stopped at a stone obelisk that stood at the entrance to the camp. Richard hadn't noticed it until now. It stood about four feet tall and appeared to be made of marble. On top of the memorial was a bronze plaque with an inscription. Pennington stared at it like he had never read it before. His countenance fell, and his head hung low as he reached out to touch the bronze top plate.

"He seems to like you," Jenny said breaking his train of thought, "Richard Alexander." Richard turned his attention back to Jenny.

"Very funny, Jenny."

"Let's go before you decide to go crazy on me and dye your hair or grow a beard. Besides, you can't afford to be late to another meeting," she said playfully.

Pennington's speech was inspirational. Clearly, he had recovered from his somber moment at the memorial. Also clear was his dedication for the children who attended his camp. Richard had learned to keep shifting his focus and avoid looking at anyone in the eye, but every once in a while, differing voices echoed in his head.

After Mr. Pennington dismissed the group, he waved his hand at Richard summoning him to a nearby worn picnic table. Richard sat across from Mr. Pennington.

"Tell me about yourself, Richard."

"There's not much to tell really. I grew up in Atlanta. My dad owns an investment firm, and my mom does a lot of charity organization work."

"And what does Richard Alexander do?"

Richard smiled and glanced at Pennington's eyes, but then quickly dropped his focus back down on his hands. He had found a small twig lying on the table that he fidgeted with to keep his eyes off Pennington's face. Mr. Pennington didn't budge making Richard more than a little uncomfortable.

"I went to the University of Pennsylvania and I work at a marketing firm in Atlanta."

"Good school. Is that where you met Jenny?"

"Yes sir. She has been a good friend."

"Richard, I adore these kids, and this camp has a reputation to uphold. Normally, I like to have more background information on the people we have here.

"I completely understand," Richard replied stopping short from finishing his sentence.

"But time is running short, and Jennifer vouches for you. Her word goes a long way with me."

Richard nodded and glanced up once more to make momentary eye contact as Pennington continued.

"You can stay here as long as you are help. I will ask Greg and Jennifer to keep an eye on you. Some of these kids have very special needs, so you can only interact with them in a group setting, understand?"

"Yes sir."

"Any questions for me?"

Richard looked up and scanned the surroundings.

"I've never seen anything like this before. It's a spectacular environment. Jenny told me that these kids are really sick..."

"Yes, they are," Pennington replied.

"And that you provide all of this for them at no cost."

"Yes, I do."

"If you don't mind me asking... why?"

Pennington bowed his head slightly and looked toward the table surface. His countenance turned from serious to sorrowful. He paused for a moment to search deep within his memory and to formulate his answer. He looked up slowly. His eyes were filling with tears, but he managed to keep them from running down his wrinkled face.

"I had a son once," he said softly. His voice crackled and he was visibly shaken. "My son was born with an abnormality; it killed him at a very young age. These children have abnormalities, too. My son met death because of great strength, but through their weaknesses, these kids find life. That is why this camp is here, and that is why I do what I do."

Pennington stood up and walked back up the hill as Richard sat silent and still for a moment not knowing exactly what Mr.

Pennington meant with that statement. Richard then stood up and walked up the hill to the memorial to satisfy his curiosity. The inscription read:

For my son, so small, so strong.
My time with you was not long.
May your death and may my tears
Help those here to overcome their fears.
I love you John.

Chapter 15

Tom Marshall Monitor Log Personal File AJMH96

It felt good to be back in the game. The flight to Philadelphia was quiet and awkward. As much as George tried to pull us together as a team, there were too many personality differences to deal with in such a short amount of time. I discovered that General Corbin's minions were named Jackson and Stewart. I assume those are their last names. It was the only way the General addressed them. They complied with every order he barked without fail. It made me glad I didn't choose the military career path that I had once entertained. Stewart was the one who gave me some insight into the General's past, but after that he wouldn't talk to me much at all. In fact, much of my conversation with either of them was met with a "no sir," "yes sir," or complete silence.

Once in Philadelphia, we set up a small war room in an old tax building on Market Street. It wasn't quite as nice as my old office building, but it had lights, air conditioning, and internet access, so we made it work. I immediately claimed an abandoned office with a window on the street side of the building. Later in the day, I regretted that decision as the traffic became a distraction. At any rate, it was a temporary location, and I wasn't planning on being there very long.

Clearly, I was not the only one who had an agenda. The General and his two partners quickly stowed their traveling gear and appeared ready to depart again.

George arranged for all of our files and data to be transported with us. As soon as we got settled in, he called a preliminary briefing meeting to set some expectations. Although George had brought some support help with us to Philadelphia, they were busy bringing in boxes of supplies and getting our computer systems online. The General, Jackson, Stewart, George, and I were the only ones in the conference room.

"Gentlemen, we need to handle this situation with a sense of urgency and the utmost of care. This is unchartered territory for all of us. If we have any chance of successfully diffusing this, we will need to work as a team. That means we keep each other updated with the latest information no matter how trivial it may seem. It also means that we stay in touch and communicate our whereabouts. I know that each of you has specific talents for this mission and that you have a lot of work to do, so I won't keep you. Let's stay in touch and focused on the same goal. Thank you for your time and effort here."

The General stood first, followed immediately by Stewart and Jackson. They all left the room without offering a hint of compliance to George's request. I have profiled and studied people for a long time, and something just doesn't sit right with this group. It could be that I was harboring some bitter personal feelings based on our first meeting, but I tried not to dwell on it very long.

"Tom," George said after waiting a few moments for the military rigidness to leave the room, "what do you recommend as our first step here?"

"Richard went to school here," I replied. "I have a couple of people that I would like to track down and talk to." I knew about Jennifer, and she was high on my list of connections to make. I trusted George, but wasn't willing to divulge all of the information I knew just yet. It was important to stay guarded about what I knew to keep the General's force tactics at bay.

Just as I finished my sentence, Stewart appeared at the door. He was stiff with his arms down at his side like he was standing at attention. We both looked up at him as an awkward silence filled the room. He may have stood there for hours if George didn't finally address him.

"Mr. Stewart, what can we do for you?" George asked calmly.

"The General will be at Fort Dix for the remainder of today." He never made eye contact with either of us.

"And I assume both of you will be joining him?" George asked almost in a taunting way.

"Yes sir," Stewart replied still with his focus fixed on the wall behind us. "We are gathering the riot gear supplies that the General requested."

"Very good," said George nodding to provide him permission to leave.

I was certain that it was George who had requested the riot gear in our meeting in Atlanta. A string of sarcastic remarks flooded my mind, but I chose not to voice any of them. At least the military presence would be stifled for the rest of the day. Fort Dix was about an hour away from our temporary home base location, and there was plenty for me to do without feeling like they were constantly looking over my shoulder.

"I would like to head over to the university to see if Richard may have contacted some old friends." I wanted to respect George's request without revealing my suspicions. I felt confident that if Richard was still hiding out in the area, I would be the first to find him.

"That's fine, Tom," George said accepting my generic plan to proceed forward. "Let me know what you find."

The University was less than a mile away from our home base. It was always beautiful this time of year. The campus buildings had a colonial architecture, and since the semester had just started, there was plenty of activity in the area. I made my way down the list talking to some of Richard's old professors and friends but came up empty at every turn. It was getting late by the time I had finished walking all of the Wharton buildings where Richard might have shown up. I had planned on visiting the park and some of the athletic fields, but they were on the other side of the campus property. Jennifer's apartment was a much shorter walk and the timing was right for her to be home.

The apartment buildings were white with red trim and matched nicely with the overall colonial feel of the campus. I approached the narrow building and knocked firmly on the door. After a few moments of silence, I knocked again, but there was no answer.

Just as I was about to give up, a door on the adjacent building opened. A girl with short brown hair came out holding an oversized purse, books, and a key ring. She closed the door behind her and inserted her key to lock it as she glanced my way.

"Hey, you looking for Jenny?"

"Yes, do you know where I can find her?"

"She's not here," the girl replied finally extracting her key after struggling with the lock.

That much, I already knew.

"Do you know where she is?" I asked.

"The middle of nowhere. She went to some camp for sick kids. She asked me to get her mail until Tuesday, so I assume she will be back then."

"Thanks. Do you know where the camp is?"

"Sure don't. Sorry."

"Do you know when she left?"

"Her and her friend left together the other day."

"Her friend?"

"Yeah, some guy I haven't seen before. I figured they were carpooling."

"Thanks."

"No problem," she said as she turned to walk away.

The biomedical library behind the hospital was my last stop for the day. Jennifer spent quite a bit of time there and was always friendly to the staff. On the way to the library, George called me to tell me that the stolen car had been found in a mall parking lot. He described it as "fairly beat up" on the inside and littered with food and candy wrappers. I tried to remain short in my conversation with George, but he seemed to know me well enough to sense that I was withholding information.

"So Tom, what is it you're not telling me?" George asked as if he was secretly tracking my every move. I hesitated. I felt like I could trust George, but I also knew that his loyalty was to the mission and that included keeping General Corbin informed of any pertinent data. I made my best attempt at dancing around his questions before I finally confessed to the relentless voice on the phone.

"Okay George, I'm chasing down a lead. I think Richard came here and found some help from an old friend. I am working on the details and may have a location within the next hour."

"That's great work, Tom. Why didn't you tell me this sooner?"

"Honestly, I don't think we need the military involvement in this. No one knows Richard better than I do. I have profiled him for years..."

"Tom, I understand where you are coming from," George interrupted, "but we've already had this conversation, and we need to follow orders on this one." George didn't know any other way. He was loyal to his job and played everything by the book.

"Our clients need to be handled carefully," I retorted. "Brute force tactics are going to lead to dangerous situations. It's just stupid."

"Sometimes Tom, we need to let stupidity run its course. Common sense will prevail."

"I hear you, George. Listen, I'm running out of daylight here. I'll call you in the morning before we head out."

"Okay, Tom, talk to you then."

I couldn't win the argument over the phone. George was much more of a personable debater. My focus was entirely on getting the detailed data I needed. Dealing with George would have to wait until the morning.

Tom Marshall Monitor Log Personal File AJMH96

End of Record

Chapter 16

We all gathered in the makeshift conference room just after sunrise. As I expected, George called General Corbin last night, and he had changed his plans to go back to Fort Dix today. I also noticed that he brought more soldiers with him this morning. They all looked very young and wore the same military green camouflage outfits. There was no doubt these guys were on loan from some of the General's local friends. It made me wonder what else the General had acquired yesterday while I was out doing the real work.

The borrowed military hands waited in the lobby area with Jackson while Stewart joined us in the conference room for the debriefing. Just like the good old days, George greeted everyone with a handshake and a warm smile.

"Good morning gentlemen," he began. "Thanks to Tom, we made some great progress yesterday, and we are fairly certain that we have a location on Richard."

"Fairly certain?" the General interrupted. "We're going to need something better than 'fairly certain'. When will we have a confirmed location on the target?"

"He's not a target..." I began to retort until George interrupted me.

"We believe Richard is held up at a camp site approximately five hours south of here. We will be leaving in just a few minutes. Let's all remember that this situation needs to be handled peacefully and quietly. Any major distractions or incidents could jeopardize the secrecy of the mission."

It was clear that the General was tuning out most of what George was saying, but he stayed quiet the remainder of the meeting, so I decided not to stir the pot.

"I'll give you a few minutes to pack up any necessary supplies. Tom and I will lead the way in our car, and you can follow," George said making eye contact with the General.

As the General stood, Stewart followed, and they both left the room. George stayed behind waiting to give me the talk about teamwork and positive attitude. I stayed behind to reiterate my opinion about how this whole mission was being handled. Once we were both comfortable that the military escort was out of ear shot, I turned my head to look at George.

"Why did you have to call them? We could have handled this."

"Tom, you know the protocol for this mission includes military support if we end up needing it. What we don't need is to keep having the same discussion. We have orders to follow, and we need to follow them."

"Must you always follow the rules?" I asked. My tone was light enough to play it off like banter but with a hint of seriousness. George was packing up some notes and papers in his briefcase. He responded without looking up at me.

"Actually no, Tom. I don't always follow the rules."

That was not the answer I was expecting. Curiosity radiated through my face. My expression shouted while my mouth stayed shut. George didn't hide anything from us; it wasn't in his character to do so. Or, maybe he did have something to hide. If that was the case, he was very good at it. My drive to dig deeper was abruptly stopped by his next words.

"Another time, another place, Tom. Right now, we need to do what we need to do." George looked up with a small grimace on his face. It seemed like he wanted to trust me with something, but for George, some discussions are meant for the rocking chair on his front porch. I sensed that this was one of those conversations. George grasped his briefcase firmly and walked to the front door, gently touching my shoulder on the way out.

"Let's go find our friend Richard," he said.

I smiled knowing that, even if the General didn't understand, George did. We considered the elite our friends. We spent our lives protecting them and caring for them. It was important to help them when they were in trouble. It was encouraging to hear George call Richard our friend.

I walked out right behind him and stopped in my temporary office to grab my backpack before heading out the front door to our car. George wasn't far behind me. Parallel parked on the street in front of the building was an ugly dark green military transport truck. Jackson was behind the steering wheel, and the General was sitting in the passenger side. I assume that Stewart and the borrowed hit men were in the back of the truck but didn't bother to ask or to look for myself. Ignoring them was easier than the thought of tolerating them.

Chapter 17

Tom Marshall Monitor Log Personal File APRV37

(cont.)

George kept the conversation superficial on the way to the camp. I made several attempts to steer the conversation back to work, but George was much too strategic for me. I finally gave in and got a full update on Danielle and each of their adult children. George loved to talk about his family. It seemed as though the only time I got a word in was to relay the GPS directions as the appointed trip navigator.

It was after noon when we arrived at the campsite. George pulled our car all the way up to the entrance of the camp while the military truck stopped short of the parking area almost blocking off the only road to get to the camp. George and I both stepped out of our vehicle and began walking down the large path in the center of the two wooden buildings.

A young man with a clipboard in his hand was walking up the hill from the lake toward us. He had short dark hair and a charming smile.

"Good afternoon," he said. "What can I help you with?"

"We're here looking for a friend of ours," George said politely, "Richard Hall."

"Doesn't sound familiar," he said pointing to the larger of the two wooden buildings on the right, "but if you step in here, we can get you to sign our guest log and see if your friend is registered."

Just as he was speaking, an older gentleman appeared from the cabin he was pointing to.

"Can we help you gentlemen?"

"Yes," George replied still with an inviting smile on his face, "we are looking for a man named Richard who may be here with his friend Jennifer Stokes."

The old man was Mr. Pennington. He moved slowly and gracefully toward us from the steps in front of the cabin. The military truck was far enough in his peripheral vision that he didn't notice it.

"Ah, yes," Mr. Pennington replied, "please step inside. We'll get you signed in and page Richard over the radio."

George was quick with a response. "Actually sir, we would like to go see him if at all possible."

"Is he in some sort of trouble?" Mr. Pennington asked.

"I am sorry, sir. I'm afraid that's all I can tell you for now. If you could please just point us in his direction, we can spend a few minutes talking to him and minimize any disturbance to the fine camp you have going on here."

Mr. Pennington was a bit perplexed but responded in a polite and compliant manner. "Of course. We do still need you to sign our visitor log just inside. It's standard policy."

"Certainly," George replied as he began walking toward the cabin.

Tom Marshall Monitor Log File APRV37
Remainder of Record Deleted

Neither George nor Tom noticed the group of young girls coming out of the mess hall walking down toward the lake. One of the group leaders was Jennifer who spotted them talking with Pennington. She froze in her tracks, and the anxiety on her face caused a great deal of concern from the other group leader.

"Are you okay, Jenny?" she said.

"Um... yes, fine. I need to go take care of something real quick. Can you please take the girls down to the lake? I'll be right there."

"Sure thing, Jenny."

Jennifer searched the crowd down by the lake. After only a few seconds, she made eye contact with Richard. She stared at him as if she were screaming her thoughts in his direction.

Richard was at the edge of the lake surrounded by more than fifty kids and counselors. He looked up to catch Jennifer's eyes and immediately heard her plea.

"Richard, there are two guys here. I think they are looking for you."

A sharp pain penetrated the right side of Richard's head just behind his eye. He winced but kept his left eye focused on Jenny's silhouette.

"Go to the girl's compound cabin number thirty-nine. My bag is in the back right corner…car keys in the front pocket…"

Richard couldn't stand the pain anymore. He closed both his eyes and put his hands over his face. He had gotten enough of the message and with his right eye still closed in pain, he ran toward one of the more shaded paths that led to the girls' compound.

Just as Jennifer had finished her mental message to Richard, a familiar voice interrupted her focus.

"Jennifer."

She turned around to respond to Mr. Pennington just as George and Tom were walking into the cabin. Pennington's call made them stop at the door. George looked at Tom as if to confirm that the young lady who had caught Pennington's attention was the Jennifer they were looking for. Tom nodded in confirmation.

"Jennifer, these gentlemen would like to speak to you for a quick minute please."

"Yes sir, Mr. Pennington." Jenny began walking toward them. She was hesitant, but she made every attempt to act natural.

George, Pennington, and Tom all walked in the cabin with Jennifer following right behind them. She walked through the door silently with a nervous smile. Her straight brown hair was pulled back in a ponytail, and her pale complexion revealed the beads of sweat on her forehead. Anxiety filled her eyes.

"Hello Jennifer, my name is Tom Marshall. We understand that Richard came here with you."

"Yes sir." Her voice was shaky. Jennifer was always safe and conservative. The thought that she might be in serious trouble made her whole body tremble. She did the best she could to hide it by folding her arms close to her body, but whatever nervousness she tried to conceal came out in her face.

Tom guessed that Richard had confided in Jennifer so easing her anxiety and keeping her close was the safest choice. "There's nothing to worry about. We just need to talk to you and Richard for a few minutes."

Both Tom and George waited for her to respond, but she stood silent with tears slowly welling up in her eyes. The awkward silence was suddenly broken by the piercing sound of gun fire and yelling. Just outside the cabin, Richard bolted from amidst the brush and ran full speed toward Jennifer's car. To his credit, the General had predicted this possibility and had gunmen poised and ready to fire.

After the first gunshot, Tom grabbed George and threw him to the ground. Richard had emerged from the trees between the

141

cabin and the General's small military team, and the cabin was taking friendly fire. The gun shots continued to pierce the air. Tom heard a scream and turned to see Jennifer grasping her left arm just above the elbow. Blood seeped from between her fingers and tears flowed freely down her face. Pennington had crouched down below the window that faced the parking lot. He was shocked but unhurt. The twenty seconds of gunfire felt as though it lasted for several minutes.

As suddenly as it had started, the gunfire stopped. Tom and George could both hear Jackson yelling commands for Richard to surrender. Tom motioned for George to attend to Jennifer while he scrambled toward the door. He slowly poked his head out the door to assess the situation. The dark green military truck was still parked facing toward the cabin blocking half of the road. In front of the truck were four young men with semi-automatic guns held up and ready to fire. The guns were pointed at the row of cars in the field. Richard had made it to Jennifer's car and was crouched down next to the driver's side door.

Sweat dripped from Richard's forehead and the sting of the bullets was scattered down the left side of his body. Though none of them penetrated his tough skin, they still throbbed and left welts where they hit. The only thing shielding him from the spray of bullets was the blue Honda that Jennifer had parked next to. He knew that he had to disable the gunmen if he had any chance of making it out.

Jackson yelled once more for Richard to stand up and surrender. The gunmen were poised and ready to fire. George had moved Jennifer to a safer place behind the counter in the cabin, and Pennington was now on his feet peering out the window. Tom stood in the doorway still watching and waiting for the next move to be made. The air was thick with tension as the standoff continued. It seemed as though everyone was waiting for someone else to make a move.

Richard was panicked but tried to keep his thoughts straight. Jackson motioned for the gunmen to move forward; guns still held high. They took five steps and stopped. Richard squatted between the two cars and reached as far as he could underneath the frame of the Honda. With a grunt, he thrust his body up and forward. The Honda went flying through the air flipping over and over as it soared toward the military truck. Jackson and the gunmen scattered as the airborne vehicle came crashing down toward them. The car landed on its left side with the roof smashed against the front bumper of the truck. Before they could get back up from the ground, Richard had jumped in Jennifer's car and raced toward the wreckage. Jackson grabbed his gun but didn't have time to shoot before the car passed at full speed. Just as suddenly as the violent encounter began, it was over. Jennifer's car left only a trail of dust and the demolished Honda lay smoking next to the military truck. None of the General's men seemed to be hurt, but they were all shocked by the encounter.

Tom glanced over at Mr. Pennington who stood motionless still staring out the window. His jaw had dropped slightly, and a single tear ran down his cheek and silently fell on the aged hardwood floor.

Chapter 18

Jennifer had been crying for almost an hour straight. The intensity changed periodically, but her eyes seemed to be an endless well of water. Her cheeks were blotchy red and moist as she laid on the makeshift gurney in the medical tent. Her tears were difficult to interpret. It may have been because of her broken heart for Richard or the disappointment she felt in herself toward Mr. Pennington, but it was certainly caused by much more than the bullet wound in her arm.

Pennington put the entire camp compound on lock down. All the children and most of the counselors were restricted to their cabins until further notice. The few counselors who were not assigned to cabins were attending to Jennifer's arm. They had managed to stop the bleeding, but they didn't have the right tools to extract the bullet lodged near the bone in her arm.

Just outside the camp, the General and his men were cleaning up the wreckage left from Richard's escape. Mr. Pennington sat on the front steps of the cabin staring in their direction but not really looking at them. George walked up behind him in an attempt to console him but before he could open his mouth, Mr. Pennington spoke.

"You need to leave," he said quietly still staring off into space.

"Yes sir. Mr. Pennington, I..."

"I don't want to hear it. I know who you people are, and I don't want anything to do with your agenda." His tone was emotionless, and his face was expressionless. "You and your friends need to be gone within the hour."

George and Pennington were not far apart in years. Even so, Pennington's character demanded respect. George simply replied with a "Yes sir" and left the old man to work through the thoughts and feelings he had bottled up inside.

True to his word, George organized the team and they left within the hour. Tom and George drove back to Philadelphia with one extra passenger in their car, and the dented military truck following closely behind. George sat in the passenger seat and spent much of the time staring out the window.

Jennifer sat in the back seat of the car bandaged and heavily medicated to numb the pain. Her eyes were swollen, and her lips were dry and chapped. Tom glanced in the rear-view mirror hoping to get her attention so he could begin questioning her but soon realized that he missed his window of opportunity. Emotionally exhausted, she sat slumped in the back seat with her head back, her eyes closed, and her hand still on her arm. Her breath was long and consistent. Tom's interrogation would have to wait.

The first three and a half hours of the trip were totally silent. The only sound to be heard was the hum of the car on the road and the soft, steady breathing from the back seat. Just as they reached the Pennsylvania state border, Jennifer woke up from her nap. Her eyes widened as she shook the normal disorientation that accompanies waking up in strange circumstances.

"Good morning," George said turning his body in his seat.

"Hello," she said sheepishly, making eye contact with Tom in the rear-view mirror.

"Do you mind if we talk a little about Richard?" Tom asked getting straight to the point.

"What's happened to him?" She said. The tone of her voice was soft and caring.

"That's classified information and quite frankly..."

Tom was stopped short by a look from George that was so strong he could almost physically feel it hit his face. George paused only for a moment before he picked up the conversation where Tom had left off.

"Miss Stokes, I know you have been through a lot in the past few days and you may not know who to trust, but I need you to believe that we are here to help you and to help Richard."

Jennifer stayed silent but acknowledged George by nodding with her eyes fixed on his.

"We need you to tell us everything you know and everything that happened since Richard showed back up in your life. Please try to remember everything you can. The more you can tell us, the better we will be able to help."

"I just wanted to help him."

"We know," George said with a smile, "and now we need you to help us help him."

She hesitated for a moment and then started to speak. "He showed up at my front door in the middle of the night. He was tired and scared. He said he just needed a place to stay, so I let him sleep on my couch for the night. The next morning, he told me that he was on that plane that crashed in Atlanta and that something had changed. He told me that after the crash he was stronger than ever and that he could hear what people were thinking. It really freaked me out at first…"

Tom hit the brakes and pulled over to the side of the road bringing the car to an abrupt stop and forcing the military truck to pull off the road behind him. He quickly turned around in his seat.

"What did you say? What was that last part?"

"You saw what he did with that car. He said that there was something wrong with his body and…"

"No, not that," Tom interrupted for a second time, "when you said he could hear what other people were thinking."

"Yes. I didn't believe him at first, but then he showed me. It was really shocking."

Tom glanced at George who was looking at Jennifer with a perplexed face. She paused for a second before she continued with her explanation.

"He can't really control it, and it hurts him really bad. I told him that I could get him some help if he came to the camp with me. I didn't know things were going to turn out like this." She started to cry. "Mr. Pennington must be so disappointed in me. I am so sorry." The cry quickly became a sob. "I never wanted anyone to get hurt. I just wanted to help."

Her last few words were almost unrecognizable as she started to choke up, and the tears flowed freely. Tom looked back at George quite surprised at this new revelation. George reached back and touched her hand.

"Thank you, Miss Stokes. You have been a big help. We're going to get you to a doctor and make sure you are well taken care of."

"What about Richard?" she asked trying to calm herself down.

"Well, we need to find him as soon as we can. We're going to help him, too," George said with a reassuring smile.

Tom carefully merged back into traffic as the silence returned to the car once more. Jennifer remained quiet and made every attempt to regain her composure. George stayed focused on the horizon straight ahead; it was evident that he was deep in thought. Tom was focused on getting Jennifer to the hospital and then getting back to his computer and his files. There was a lot of work to do and not much time to do it.

Chapter 19

Tom Marshall Monitor Log Personal File APRV252

The General and his entourage disappeared when we got back into Philadelphia. They stayed quiet and humble as if coming home empty handed from a hunting trip. George stayed with Jennifer at the hospital to make sure she was taken care of and that the local authorities didn't start asking a lot of questions while I went back to our headquarters to do some research. George and I didn't get a chance to talk about the information that Jennifer shared, but I could tell by the look on his face that this was something he had never encountered before.

My research quickly confirmed this event as an anomaly. In all of the records I had access to, nothing like this was ever documented. All the way back to the beginning of the monitor department, there was no indication of a similar situation. Never before had one of the elite been identified as having crossed class boundaries. It just wasn't possible; at least that is what we thought. I knew I wouldn't be able to sleep that night, so I made myself comfortable in front of the computer and started to dig.

Hours passed and the words on the screen started to blur. I looked through records, websites, and medical history for everyone and everything associated with Richard. Finally, I found something that was hidden by the Hall family from a long time ago.

William and Caroline Hall met at a business party. William already had a great start in his career with a large inheritance he received from his father. He used that inheritance to make some risky investments that paid off. He climbed the corporate ladder quickly, and his wealth increased exponentially. Caroline was a summer intern at the same company. She had seen friends and family struggle with finances, and she had promised herself that she would do whatever it took to make sure that she could live in luxury for the rest of her life. Her ticket to that dream was William.

If William knew that her motivation in life was status, he didn't let it bother him. For William, attracting the attention of a pretty girl ten years younger than him was reason enough to strike up a conversation. Caroline quickly threw herself into the wealthy lifestyle and played the part flawlessly. On the outside, everything seemed perfect. On the inside, her insecurities became her demons. Caroline didn't let anything distract her from maintaining the picture-perfect lifestyle that she loved.

When several of their socialite friends became pregnant, William and Caroline followed. It seemed like the perfect pregnancy. She had magazine-worthy baby showers and the latest fashion maternity clothes. She was cute and glamorous in the public eye, but behind closed doors, she held a secret. It was a secret she kept hidden so well that it slipped through our systems entirely.

It wasn't difficult to keep the secret from William. He never had time to join her for doctor's visits. There always seemed to be a business crisis to deal with. Instead, she bore the burden alone.

Caroline was stunned at her first ultrasound visit to discover that she was carrying twins. She was equally stunned when the doctor delivered the bad news; one of her babies was not developing properly. The pregnancy became categorized as high risk and from that point, she paid to have private consultation visits with a personal physician.

As the pregnancy continued, she was informed that one of the babies was a boy and the other a girl. The boy seemed to be developing normally with only a few complications. The girl remained very small. Her heartbeat was distinguishable but weak, and she wasn't growing. For the remaining months, Caroline continued the façade. Fearing that she would only deliver one healthy baby, she never told anyone about the twin girl struggling to survive inside her womb. As the delivery date grew near, prenatal tests indicated that both babies were strong candidates for the restrainer chip.

Consistent with his character, William was busy when Caroline went into labor. She had already arranged a private room with a dedicated personal staff of doctors and nurses. Richard was born first and was quickly whisked away for a restrainer chip implant. As expected, the second baby had not survived. The doctors were uncertain when the little heartbeat failed to keep beating, but they suspected it was only a few weeks before Caroline went into labor. Caroline felt ashamed and distressed. She did everything possible to cover up the existence of the second baby. She didn't want to be viewed as a failure in the eyes of their shallow friends.

It took her several months to fully regain control of her emotions. She was quickly diagnosed with postpartum depression and was prescribed a significant dosage of medication. As the sands of time and the bottles of pills passed, she suppressed the memory so deep in her mind that it became nothing more than a forgotten nightmare. Her recovery was aided by a consuming focus on Richard. After his chip implant, Richard developed normally and grew up to be a handsome and popular young man. Caroline sometimes treated him like a trophy when it was convenient for her social circles.

William also took great pride in their son but maintained his focus on work. He hired the best nannies to raise Richard and provided for all of his needs and wants. On occasion, William would try to convince Caroline to have a second child so that Richard would have someone to play with. Caroline refused to entertain the thought and William never knew why.

Richard's twin sister would have been categorized as a Class 2 elite. Although I had extensive training in human anatomy, I still didn't understand much about genetics or prenatal development. I couldn't be entirely sure that Richard's sister somehow played a part in his unique development, but it was the only link I had. Nothing else had any probable chance of making sense. I sat and pondered the possibilities for what seemed like hours. Finally, my eyes became heavy and my brain became tired. It was very late, and the couch in the lobby made for a decent bed for the remaining hours of the night.

I awoke to the sound of George coming in the front door. He gave me a perplexed look as he approached.

"What?" I said sitting up on the couch, "Are you really surprised to find me here?"

George grinned sarcastically. "No, not surprised at all. Rough night?"

"Yes. How's Jennifer?"

"She is going to be fine. She just needs some time to heal."

"How bad was the arm?"

"Not as bad as it looked. She got lucky with that one. Unfortunately, her arm isn't the biggest wound that needs to heal. She's been through quite a lot. I'm going to stay close to her to help her recover until we get a solid lead on Richard. Any ideas on where he is heading next?"

George's compassion was evident in his eyes. I felt like there was some interaction with him and Jennifer that he wasn't telling me about, but I didn't press the issue. Maybe he wanted to keep her close in case Richard tried making contact again. Nevertheless, there were bigger issues to focus on.

"No, but I do have some interesting news to share."

"Well then," George said with his typical grimace, "let's get back to work."

George and I walked back to my temporary office where I showed him the results of my all-night research blitz. He was just as shocked as I was.

"Is it really possible?" George asked rhetorically.

"It's just a theory, but it's the only explanation that has any merit. I couldn't find any documentation of a similar case."

"No, there hasn't been. I have been working for the department since the beginning, and I have never seen anything like this. How did we not know about this?"

I didn't have any good answers. Much like George, all I had were more questions. My head was spinning and still a bit groggy from lack of sleep.

"This may complicate matters," George said as he stood up to leave. "Good work on this, Tom. We'll meet with the team at ten this morning. In the meantime, please keep me up to date on what you find."

"Will do."

"And Tom…don't plan on staying late today. You need to catch up on some rest."

He was right. I was tired. The excitement and adrenaline rush that came as a result of my research was fading, but the perplexity wasn't. I was anxious to have another encounter with Richard. Armed with this new data, I wanted to talk to him and to study him. I wanted more information, but my body just wanted sleep.

Tom Marshall Monitor Log Personal File APRV252
End of Record

Chapter 20

Two weeks passed slowly. Tom's one and only encounter with Richard since the accident fell short of expectations, but he wasn't giving up. He was linked in to every news station and every police database within a two hundred mile radius of the campsite. With each passing day, Tom expanded the perimeter of his search looking for any criminal activity or strange events. Richard managed to keep himself out of the spotlight, but it was only a matter of time before his extraordinary abilities and desperate situation would lead him to do something newsworthy.

The office complex was cold and quiet. The temperatures outside dropped a little each day and the temporary headquarters for the team lacked robust insulation. The General and his men came in and out periodically but remained silent most of the time which was more than satisfactory for Tom. After the last encounter with Richard, he began to wonder if the General's tactics might actually be needed, but he refused to show anything but disdain for the General and his men. The lack of respect was quite mutual. The whole team was just frustrated. Everyone waited for the inevitable but illusive confrontation with Richard.

At George's prompting, Tom went with him to visit Jennifer once she was discharged from the hospital. Ashley and her son Joshua drove up to stay with her for a few days to help cheer her up. They had stayed at the camp for the rest of the week to help with the kids. Ashley reassured her that everything at the camp was fine after the incident and that Mr. Pennington wasn't angry with her. She needed to hear that.

Despite Tom's impolite treatment of her when they first met, she greeted him with a warm smile and a courteous but feminine handshake. "Mr. Marshall, I am so sorry again for…"

"No need to apologize, Jennifer," he said as she invited George and Tom into her apartment. Ashley and Joshua were both in the kitchen to their right as they entered. The floor plan was open but cozy having only a half wall and countertop separating the kitchen and the living room.

"Please have a seat. I don't know what else I can tell you about Richard, but I am okay talking about it now."

"Thank you, Jennifer," George said as they both sat on the same couch where Richard laid his head. "We can't stay long, but we just wanted to drop in and check on you."

"Do you have any idea where he might have gone?" Tom said, still preoccupied with finding Richard. George looked at him with a subtle disapproval of the question. Clearly there was a lesson in the importance of relationship versus business that George was trying to teach Tom, but he was way too uncomfortable with relationships and way too comfortable with business to change his tactics.

"I'm afraid I don't," she replied looking down at her feet. The shame of sadness started to show on her face, and she fought hard to keep it suppressed. "I wish I knew where he was. I could help you look for him. I know that he is hurting, and I really want to help in any way I can."

"I appreciate your offer," George said with a grin, "but we really need to take care of it from here. There is something I need you to do though." Jennifer nodded in agreement. "This is a sensitive situation that, quite frankly, we don't fully understand yet. The best way to help protect Richard is to keep what you have seen and heard to yourself for now. We don't want to put anyone in harm's way."

"Of course. Not a problem."

George glanced over at Ashley and Joshua still working in the kitchen. Ashley didn't say a word but nodded that she understood and would also comply with the request.

Joshua was a quiet, skinny kid who looked strangely familiar to Tom. He made the connection when Joshua turned around revealing a small scar on the back of his neck. His short haircut made it easy to spot, and Tom instantly recognized it as a restrainer chip implant. Tom looked him up in the database later to confirm his suspicions and discovered that he was a Class 2 elite, a healer. If he wasn't restrained, he could have helped his

161

friend Jennifer with her wounded arm, but he could not have fixed her broken heart.

George shifted his weight forward on the couch and began to stand up. "And now, Miss Stokes, we do need to leave. Thank you for your hospitality."

Jennifer stood and walked them to the front door. She shook Tom's hand first and said "goodbye." He walked out the door with George following behind. Just before George stepped out, Jennifer grabbed his arm and whispered, "Please don't let anything bad happen to Richard. Please promise me."

"I'll do my best to take care of him," George said.

Jennifer stood at the door and watched them leave. She kept her smile and eyes fixed on the car until they turned the corner. Despite her emotional trauma, she seemed to be in good spirits.

As they drove away, Tom asked George about Jennifer's unusually peaceful attitude, but he didn't say anything more than "sometimes people find true hope only after they hit rock bottom."

After enduring awkward silence day after day, Tom finally picked up a lead in the form of an alert from Charlotte, North Carolina. He almost chuckled under his breath when he first read the report. It was a bank robbery. It seemed a bit old fashion and almost escaped notice, but there were some unique circumstances behind this particular incident. The theft happened at night when no one was around. The vault has been compromised from the outside of the building with a couple of sledgehammers and a six-inch diameter solid steel bar. All of the tools had been left at the scene with no fingerprints to speak of.

The more Tom read, the more certain he was that this was the responsibility of Richard. Tom notified George who made the call that it was time to move the operation south. He let Tom leave immediately so he could get to the crime scene as quickly as possible while the rest of the team prepared to mobilize.

Tom's mind kept churning on the way down to Charlotte. As requested, the local authorities left the crime scene undisturbed. It was an impressive display of destruction. Richard had demolished the exterior wall of the building as well as the concrete wall of the vault. It appeared as though he used the large steel bar as a lever to create a hole in the rebar mesh within the destroyed concrete wall. The hole was just large enough for one person to wiggle in and then back out again.

The damaged exterior wall was located opposite the road. Camera footage revealed a masked man driving up behind the building in an old pickup truck with the eight feet long steel bar in the truck bed. Because of the camera angle, there wasn't a good shot of the actual break in, but Tom pieced together the events in the most logical manner.

After dodging some of the questions from the local authorities, Tom discovered that there had only been thirteen minutes between the alarm trigger and the arrival of the police on the scene. By the time they arrived, the criminal was already gone leaving only a trail of rubble and tools of destruction behind. Richard had done his homework. He knew how to use his strength to his advantage. He knew where to get in, what to go after, and how much time it would take. He also knew that someone was still chasing him. His trail of broken concrete and tools left no clue about his next move.

George, the General, and the rest of the team traveled back to Atlanta. It was a perfect central location to the area where they thought Richard would stay. Although Richard endured the cold weather of Pennsylvania during his college years, Tom knew that Richard hated the snow and ice of the north. With winter approaching, a warmer climate would make Richard feel more comfortable in his new life as a fugitive. He was also much more familiar with the territory and environment of the Atlanta area.

After the bank incident, the action stopped. Much like the weather, the trail for Richard had turned cold.

With each passing day, Richard had more time to plan his strategy and more time to get familiar with his power. He trained himself to evade the eyes of other people. He learned to focus on tuning out the voices and avoiding the corresponding pain. Each day he gained more control, and each day the team lost more of an advantage. It was clear that Richard wanted to stay hidden, and Tom feared that he was planning something big, but as hard as he tried to anticipate the next incident, no one could have predicted the episode that was about to take place.

Chapter 21

Christina Monroe looked at the clock again. "Wow, this day is dragging on," she murmured to herself. She had a modest job running medical lab samples for a company called Flint Chemical based in Atlanta. The lab was located in a narrow rented building on South Hill Street in downtown Griffin, Georgia. It was a job she enjoyed, but today it was hard to stay focused. She glanced at the clock again.

"You know, Chrissy, you can't make time go any faster by staring down the clock," said her coworker. Christina smiled, acknowledging Holly's observation.

"You noticed?" Christina replied sheepishly, while glancing back at the clock.

"Please," Holly replied playfully rolling her eyes, "as if I could miss it; you have been looking at that clock every minute or so for the last hour. If I didn't know any better, I would think you had a hot date tonight."

Christina's smile grew larger. "As a matter of fact, I do. Jacob and I are celebrating our wedding anniversary tonight, and we are going to Baldomeros for dinner."

"I heard that it's amazing; I can't wait to hear all about it," Holly said. "Maybe one day I'll have a man who loves me like Jacob loves you. Heck, at this point I would be happy with a man who would just take me on a date to Baldomeros." Both women laughed. Holly was ten years older than Christina but had never found the right man to settle down with.

"One day, Holly, you will have a great man who will love you more than you could ever imagine."

Holly smiled, "Thanks but for now I am happy living life through you and Jacob. Besides, I think my glory years are over. I am the victim of a small-town environment. There's just not enough selection around here, and I'm definitely not as lucky with love as you are."

"You know luck is only for the superstitious."

"Sure, I guess," Holly said as she left the room.

Christina allowed herself a moment to remember back to the day she first saw Jacob. It was the second day of high school. She was a senior, but it was a new school for her. She remembered it was the second day of school because she would always ask herself how she could have missed him on the first day. He had striking features but wasn't consumed by his looks. Jacob's normal attire was a pair of jeans, a t-shirt, and a baseball cap. He had a chiseled face, with a smile that could melt any young girl's heart. He had brown wavy hair that poked out from the sides of his baseball cap. He was tall and athletic with broad

166

shoulders, but it was his piercing blue eyes that Christina noticed first. As he walked toward her in the hall, his smile distracted her from switching out books at her locker and caused her to drop some of them in the process. Jacob was a complete gentleman and turned around to help. Christina smiled at the memory as she checked the clock and noticed it was 4:58. "Finally," she said to herself and then glanced around to see if anyone heard.

As she was driving home, her mind once again drifted back. "Why don't I just carry these for you to your next class," Jacob said after picking up some of her books.

Christina remembered how hot her cheeks felt during that moment, and she hoped that the makeup she was wearing would disguise the blushing. "You really don't have to do that," she replied.

Jacob looked at her with those intense blue eyes, "I really don't mind. What class do you have next?"

"Algebra," she replied, trying to remember how to breathe.

"Mr. Whatley's class," Jacob said with a grin.

Although she didn't need to take the books that Jacob had picked up for her, she still gave him a big smile and accepted his offer. "My name is Christina, what's yours?"

"Jacob Monroe," he replied. "Are you new here?" He already knew the answer to that question, but he asked it to keep the conversation going.

Still a bit embarrassed by the whole scene, Christina replied, "My mother and I just moved here from Tampa to live with my grandmother. My Dad passed away several months ago, and my mom didn't want me spending my afternoons alone while she was working." Christina remembered how Jacob turned to her and looked her directly in her eyes. She could see the sorrow in his eyes was genuine, almost as if he could feel the loss that she experienced personally.

"Try not to drop these again," Jacob said as they arrived at Mr. Whatley's class, and he handed Christina her books. "It was great meeting you. I guess I'll be seeing you around," Jacob said as a big smile formed on his face.

"Thanks again Jacob," Christina said as she watched him walk away. She wasn't sure what it was, but she knew that there was something special about Jacob Monroe, because she had never felt that way around anyone else before.

The very next Sunday, Christina and her mother visited First Baptist church on West Taylor Street and were met by a friendly lady at the door. "Good morning," she said. "My name is Suzanna Monroe. It is so good to have you here this morning. Is this your first time visiting us?" Suzanna was in her mid-fifties but still had a youthful look and a warm smile that was very recognizable. They talked for a few minutes when Christina heard a familiar voice. "Well hey there, Christina". She turned around to see Jacob, dressed in khaki slacks and a nice red polo shirt.

"Hey, Jacob!" Christina said before realizing that she sounded a bit too excited.

"My mom isn't talking your ear off, is she?" he asked as he walked up to stand next to Suzanna.

"No, not at all," Christina replied. "She was just welcoming us to your church."

"Hey, would you like me to show you where my friends and I sit?" he asked. Christina turned to her mother for approval and then headed into the sanctuary with Jacob. He was well liked by all, and he made it a point to make sure Christina met everyone.

Jacob and Christina became best friends. They both hid their feelings for each other for a while. They were both too shy to admit their attraction. Christina had only had one other boyfriend in her life. It was a short-lived relationship that left her broken hearted. She loved the way Jacob made her feel, but she was apprehensive about getting close enough for him to break her heart. Jacob had never had a serious relationship. He never wanted to date anyone that he wouldn't seriously consider marrying. Such a girl did not exist – until now.

Christina loved reminiscing about their early relationship. Jacob always thought it was silly, but he humored her nonetheless. Christina kept volumes of photo albums highlighting their relationship and experiences together. Christina always enjoyed anniversaries for the sole reason that it gave her an excuse to pull out the photo albums and just sit and talk with Jacob while they recalled their memories.

As she reached their modest home, Christina rushed out of the car and trotted inside. She knew that she didn't have much time before Jacob got home, and she wanted to look her best when he arrived.

Jacob was a common man. After high school, he attended a two-year technical school and went to work as a maintenance technician at the local industrial plant. He considered going to a four-year college but wanted to wait until he got a solid job before he married Christina, and four years just seemed too long to wait to start their married life together. Jacob was a man of faith; he was very active in his church and was firm in his convictions about God. He wasn't fanatical or freaky about his religion, but it permeated everything he did. Even if someone didn't agree with everything Jacob believed, his convictions still demanded respect.

He was a hard worker and a good student. Jacob was always the first one awake in the morning and got deep satisfaction from helping his parents out on the farm. Jacob knew what he wanted out of life. He was never enamored with fame or fortune but instead lived a simple life seeking to find true love and help others.

Jacob treated Christina like she was a princess. He worked diligently to provide for her every need. After seven years of marriage, he still looked at her like she was the prettiest girl he had ever seen.

Jacob was also watching the clock that day. He took pride in planning their anniversary dinner on his own and was anxious to see her reaction.

"Hey guys, I'll see you all tomorrow; I gotta run. I am taking my beautiful bride out on a date tonight," Jacob said as he put away his tools. Jacob was excited about the reservations he had made at Baldomeros for that night. He knew it was Christina's favorite restaurant. It was outside the boundaries of their budget to eat there, but tonight was a special occasion. If there were ever two people who were perfect for each other, it was Jacob and Christina.

Chapter 22

Christina was finishing her makeup when Jacob's dirty pickup truck pulled in the gravel driveway. She was beaming with excitement as she watched him from the window. As he got closer to the front door, Christina walked over to meet him. Her normal routine each afternoon included welcoming him home at the front door with a kiss. After seven years of marriage, she never got over the feeling of excitement when Jacob came home, and he never got tired of her kisses.

"You better hurry up and get changed," she said as he walked toward the bedroom.

"It's good to see you too sweetheart," Jacob playfully replied as he headed toward the shower.

"You know I love you, Jacob," Christina said still prodding him to hurry. Jacob loved to see her so excited.

"Yes ma'am, I do."

Jacob took a quick shower and got dressed in some of his Sunday best attire. Christina had ironed his favorite shirt and had his whole outfit laying out on the bed for him. Jacob wasn't much for matching his own clothes, but she always took care of him and made him look good. Christina was anxiously waiting by the front door when Jacob came out and stopped.

"Wow!" he said, "You are the most beautiful woman in the entire world."

Christina smiled and blushed. Her cheeks soon matched the flattering red dress she had picked out just for this occasion. He could still make her feel like she did the first time they met so many years ago.

"Thank you, Jacob", she said. "It's a good thing I got stuck with the most handsome man in the world."

Jacob grinned as he walked toward her. "Close your eyes," he said.

She loved it when he told her to close her eyes. He approached her slowly. She could feel his presence and then suddenly but smoothly his strong arms wrapping around her body. They were hands of strength and hands of comfort. "I love you," he whispered and then gently pressed his lips to hers. The kiss was short but powerful. It sent chills down her back and brought a gleaming smile to her face.

"I love you too, Jacob Monroe."

He slowly moved his hand to the small of her back as they headed out the front door and down the steps toward Christina's car.

"Do you really have to bring those?" Jacob asked pointing at the photo albums Christina held close to her chest.

"Yes," she replied. "Even though you won't admit it, you love to look at them just as much as I do."

As they approached the car, Jacob opened the door for her like he always did before walking around to the driver's side. Baldomeros was a twenty-minute drive from their home, but traffic in their small hometown usually wasn't bad. Jacob started the car and slipped in a music CD as he pulled out of the driveway. Christina smiled as her favorite song started playing. Jacob never missed the little touches. It was one of the things that kept their relationship solid. She could always count on him to remember the special little things she loved. As Jacob turned onto the expressway, Christina started flipping through the first photo album.

"I have been very excited about tonight, Jacob."

"I have too" he replied.

"I have a special surprise for you tonight," Christina said tauntingly.

"Really?" Jacob said, "I hope it isn't much more than a card, because we agreed that we didn't have money to spend on each other this year and..."

"Just wait and see", Christina said. "It didn't cost any money, but you're going to love it."

"How about a hint?" he asked.

"No way, Jacob. You are just going to have to be patient; good things come to those who wait," Christina said with a devious smile.

The expressway was a little more crowded than Jacob expected, and he was starting to get worried about being late. Christina was already deeply enthralled in the photo albums with the remains of that devious smile still on her lips.

"Remember this?" Christina asked pointing to a picture of her and Jacob hiking at Stone Mountain Park.

"I do," Jacob said as he glanced over.

"That was such a great honeymoon," she remarked, "This is one of my favorite pictures." She pulled the picture from its sleeve to admire the scenery as if she was reliving the moment.

"I wish I could have given you more."

"All I want is you," Christina replied with a smile. "You have given me everything I ever needed or wanted. You make me so happy."

"Well," Jacob said, "let's see if we can keep that trend going by getting you to your special dinner on time." He had been waiting for an opportunity to pass a tractor-trailer that was driving slowly in the left-hand lane. Finally, an opening appeared in the right lane, and Jacob cautiously switched lanes. Just as he was about to pass the truck, his left front tire blew out causing Christina's little compact car to swerve left into the front of the truck. Jacob hit the brakes but couldn't stop the car from slamming into the side of the truck cab, crushing the left front side of the vehicle. The impact of the truck jerked the car back over to the shoulder, and the rear of the car swung around. Jacob tried regaining control of the vehicle, but it was too late. Christina dropped the photo album on the floorboard and braced herself against the door with a gasp. The vehicle became airborne, flipping over and over down the road.

Plastic and metal parts were flying off the car with every roll. The screeching of tires behind them and the sound of metal colliding with asphalt was deafening. Jacob clenched the steering wheel with one hand and reached over with the other trying to protect Christina while the car rolled over and over. Christina's photo album launched up from the floor to hit her in the face and then blew out the shattered window. Jacob glanced over to see Christina's face bleeding and her head jerking at every impact. It all seemed to be happening in slow motion. He felt so helpless. He wanted to grab her and shield her from the surrounding chaos, but he couldn't move. There were so many forces pulling and pushing on both of them. Jacob was overwhelmed by the panic and fear in her eyes. Then, suddenly, everything went black.

The car finally came to a stop upside-down on the shoulder of the road. Glass and metal debris were scattered about, and the limp bodies of Jacob and Christina dangled from the seat belts.

People were rushing over to the crushed vehicle from every angle. Others were on their cell phones calling for help. The smell of burnt rubber and motor oil engulfed the scene. The truck driver pulled over and ran toward the car to help. In the distance, sirens could already be heard as bystanders stood helplessly in shock.

A fire truck was the first emergency vehicle on the scene followed shortly by an ambulance. The paramedics ran over to check Jacob and Christina who were both unconscious. The fire fighters retrieved their hydraulic cutters while the paramedics continued to check and analyze both crash victims.

Two of the fire fighters immediately began cutting through the driver's side door while two others doused the engine compartment with the full contents of a fire extinguisher. Jacob was slightly more accessible and soon he was quickly extracted from the vehicle and laid out on a gurney. Christina was still in the vehicle and had been pinned against the dashboard at her waist. The paramedics loaded Jacob in the ambulance as a second ambulance and several police cars arrived on the scene.

It took several minutes for the rescue workers to clear Christina from the wrecked car. They placed her unconscious body on a stretcher board and moved her quickly to the back of the ambulance. Despite not being a big city rescue team, the small group of professionals were focused and precise. They quickly loaded Christina in the ambulance and left the scene with sirens blaring.

Chapter 23

Suzanna took her focus off her knitting needles and glanced at the clock with a smile. It was 7:00PM, and she knew that Jacob & Christina would be at dinner by now. She wondered if Christina had already told him the good news. It was killing her not to tell anyone that she would soon be a grandmother. She felt like screaming it from the rooftop.

She sat in her recliner and lowered her project into her lap as she remembered that day several weeks ago when she was at Jacob's house to help Christina plant some flowers. She made it a habit to visit Christina when Jacob had to work on a Saturday. On that particular day, she noticed that Christina looked a little pale.

"Are you feeling okay, Chrissy?" she asked.

"I think I am fighting off a bug or something. There's been something going around. Several people in the lab have been under the weather recently. I've been feeling really sick to my stomach lately. I am not running a fever, so I don't think I'm contagious," Christina replied as she shoveled some dirt. "I just feel tired all the time. Lately, the smallest task simply wears me out."

Suzanna just listened as she took her gloves off and checked her watch. "Maybe we should call it a day. It is lunch time, so it's a perfect time to take a break".

Christina agreed. Both ladies made their way inside to clean up and make lunch. When they got to the kitchen, Suzanna headed for the refrigerator while Christina stopped at their modest little pantry to grab some bread. They worked together gathering all of the ingredients to make sandwiches, but when Christina opened the pickle jar the aroma sent her straight to the bathroom. At that moment there was no doubt in Suzanna's mind that Christina was pregnant. After a few minutes, Christina arrived back into the kitchen, and she saw her mother-in-law just smiling from ear to ear.

"I am so sorry about that. I don't know what just came over me."

"Chrissy, I don't think you are fighting a bug dear, and I don't think you caught whatever is going around. I think you may be pregnant."

Christina was stunned. They had tried to get pregnant for several years when they were first married, but after so much disappointment, they just stopped trying.

"Oh, I hadn't thought about that at all," Christina said as she let the thought sink in. "We tried for so long without... I just thought we couldn't." Christina was at a loss for words.

"There is only one way to find out for sure. Let's go. We have to run to the store," Suzanna said as she got up and reached for her purse. That afternoon their suspicions were confirmed with two pink lines. Suzanna and Christina were thrilled, and instantly Christina knew when she was going to tell Jacob.

"Mom, don't say anything. I want to wait and tell Jacob on our anniversary. It will be the best gift ever!" Suzanna kept her word and didn't say anything to anyone. It had only been a few weeks since the pregnancy test, but keeping the secret made time drag on for Suzanna. She knew Jacob would be calling soon with the news, and she could hardly wait. Just when she felt like she was going to burst with excitement, the phone rang.

"Hello," Suzanna answered with glee in her voice.

"Suzanna, it's me Marge."

"Oh hello, Marge," Suzanna said somewhat disappointed.

"Suzanna you have to come down to the hospital right now!" Marge said in a frantic voice.

Suzanna froze at the sound of those words "Marge, what's wrong?"

"Jacob and Christina were just brought in. They were in a bad accident. I told the paramedics that I knew you guys and would call you." Marge worked the front desk at the emergency room, and Suzanna knew that it was serious.

"Are they okay?" Suzanna asked as she felt her heartbeat pounding faster. The feeling of anticipation was replaced by a deep feeling of dread, and she was having a hard time making the transition.

"I don't know. They both appeared to be unconscious when they came in. Just get down here and be careful. We don't need another accident, okay?"

"Yes of course," was all Suzanna could manage to say as she hung up the phone and ran outside screaming "Robert, Robert hurry!!!"

She saw Robert walk out of the barn and toward the house. His steps quickened as he got closer and was running by the time he reached Suzanna.

"What is it Sue?"

"It's Jacob and Christina. They've been in an accident and they're at the hospital. We have to go now!" The panic was in her voice and on her face. She was shaking all over.

Robert put his hands on her shoulders and paused while he looked into her eyes. "It's okay Suzanna; they're getting the care they need right now. Let's calm down and just say a prayer before we head over there."

Suzanna was an emotional wreck. Her tear-filled eyes looked at Robert, and she struggled to find the right words.

"Take a deep breath, Sue."

She knew he was right. She had to calm down. The young couple was at the hospital which meant they were both still alive. She tried her best to take deep breaths. She bowed her head to join her husband in prayer, but she had a hard time focusing on the comforting words coming from his mouth. Her mind was racing.

They drove to the hospital in silence. Suzanna's thoughts drifted to the daughter they lost thirty-one years earlier. "Lord please. I can't lose another child. Please let them be okay, please!" She whispered. She tried to remember to breathe as she thought back to the moment they found out she was pregnant with Jacob. It was two years after losing their precious Julie. Any other couple would have been ecstatic to be pregnant, but their news came with a haunting fear. What if this baby is like Julie? Who knows how long it will live? She remembered the questions well. Although it had been many years, the fear felt familiar. There are just no words to describe the devastation of a mother who has lost a child, and the paralysis that comes with the possibility of the same ordeal a second time.

Robert was a different man after they had lost Julie. He had always been a godly man, and he treated everyone with a great deal of respect. After Julie died though, Robert became stronger. He was much more vocal about his convictions and was unwavering in his commitment to do what he believed was right. It was Robert who insisted that Jacob be born and raised in their hometown, and it was Robert who refused to let their family be captive to government control. He became a man of surrender to a higher power and a man of convictions. Through that dark valley

183

many years ago, Robert and Suzanna walked hand-in-hand. Now it seemed like they had been dropped into another dark valley. She relied on Robert's strong hands and his strong heart. As that strong hand reached over to rest on hers, Suzanna snapped back to present day and realized that they were already at the hospital. She opened the car door and walked anxiously toward the emergency room lifting up one more silent prayer to God that her children were still alive.

Chapter 24

The darkness of night overtook the hospital where Jacob and Christina lay still. Jacob arrived at the hospital first but was quickly processed, cleaned up, and assigned to a room for monitoring. It was the same hospital where he was born, though it had been refurbished and updated. There were two beds in his room separated by a beige curtain. Fortunately for the Monroe's, the hospital was lacking in activity that night which offered Robert and Suzanna room to sit.

Christina had been rushed to a surgical room and was not permitted to have visitors yet, so they both stayed in Jacob's room. There was nothing to do but pray and wait. Jacob had tubes and wires connected to his body and bandages on his head and neck. The room was still and quiet. Hours passed. Robert left a wear-mark in the floor from pacing as he prayed, and Suzanna had filled the small trash can in the room with tear-soaked tissues.

The nurse walked into Jacob's hospital room and saw his worn-out parents sitting and staring at Jacob. They hadn't moved since the last time she came to check on him. She walked over to them and in a low comforting tone said, "Mr. & Mrs. Monroe, you have been up here for hours. Why don't you go and get yourself something to eat? I really don't expect him to do much until morning, and you need to make sure you have your energy for when he wakes up."

Although Suzanna appreciated the nurse's concern, she began to insist that they stay in Jacob's room until she was stopped by Robert's eyes. He motioned for Suzanna to follow his lead. He turned to the nurse and said "You're right. Thank you." He took Suzanna's hand and said, "Let's go to the cafeteria and get something to eat. It will do us both some good."

They were gone about five minutes when Jacob regained consciousness. The hospital staff expected Jacob to wake up slowly and be groggy from the pain medication, but Jacob's body jerked into a conscious state as if he had just jumped out of a dream. His eyes opened wide and his pupils were enlarged as if they were trying to soak up as much light as possible. He woke up with a sharp headache and a deep knot in his stomach as if he knew that something was terribly wrong. He was confused about where he was and began calling out Christina's name with a heavy tone of panic and anxiety. The nurse quickly rushed in and tried to calm him down.

"Where's Chrissy?" Jacob asked.

"Calm down Mr. Monroe," she replied, "the doctor will be in to see you shortly."

"Where is my wife?" Jacob insisted, "Is she okay? What happened? I need to see her." Several of the tubes and probes connected to him were at risk of falling off as Jacob instinctively tried to sit up and get out of bed. The nurse put one hand on his forehead, wet from the cold sweat droplets of anxiety, and the other on his arm trying to get him to lay back down on the bed.

"Mr. Monroe, you were in a very serious car accident. You've been unconscious since late yesterday," the nurse replied. "I'm afraid that's all I can tell you for now. Doctor Richardson will be in soon to see you and explain some things to you. In the meantime, you've been through a lot, and we need you to rest."

Jacob wasn't satisfied with her response but reluctantly decided not to fight it anymore. Having succeeded in the battle of wills, the nurse checked the machines, the IV bag, and his vitals before leaving. The night shift crew never did get high ratings in the friendly category, but the next best choice for hospital care was over two hours away.

"I will make sure the doctor knows that you are up. He will be in to see you shortly," she said rather nonchalantly as she walked out of the room. Jacob could see her talking to a doctor outside his door and across the hall but couldn't hear what they were saying. They only talked for a minute before the doctor entered his room.

"Hello, Mr. Monroe," he said. "My name is Doctor Richardson. How are you feeling today?"

Jacob, still cold and clammy responded, "I am fine, where is Chrissy? Is she okay?"

187

"Jacob, I'm sorry. I have some bad news for you," Doctor Richardson said solemnly. A look of terror overcame Jacob's countenance as the doctor continued. "The car accident was very serious. You and your wife both sustained multiple injuries. She is alive but in serious condition. We're going to be keeping her in the intensive care unit for a few days."

Jacob was slightly relieved to hear that she was still alive, but he intuitively knew that there was more that he needed to hear.

"How bad is she hurt?" Jacob asked. The doctor hesitated. He intended to provide small bits of information to Jacob over time so he wouldn't feel overwhelmed, but Jacob sounded insistent on getting all of the facts.

"The accident separated her spinal cord. The damage was severe and un-repairable. She is paralyzed from the waist down. I am sorry Jacob; there wasn't anything we could do. She is going to need plenty of time to rest and recover."

Jacob paused. He could hear the sound of his own breathing, and his heart ached for his wife.

"When can I see her?" Jacob asked as his voice crackled.

"Jacob, there's one more thing that you need to know," Dr. Richardson said as he took a deep breath before continuing. "We couldn't save your baby; I am so sorry."

"What?"

"The damage to your wife's abdomen was considerable, and it was too late by the time they arrived at the hospital."

Jacob was horrified. He felt like his whole world had been turned upside down. That was her surprise. He would have never guessed. His first thought was to blame himself; maybe if he had gotten home sooner, or maybe if he had just stayed behind that truck. The scenarios consumed him and left him speechless. There was a void in the pit of his stomach. He felt a deep loss for a child that he didn't even know existed, and he felt anguish for his beautiful wife who would be confined to a wheelchair the rest of her life. None of this seemed fair. Finally, after several moments of rushing thoughts and what-if scenarios, his mind went blank. Jacob lay motionless in the bed and wept.

A few minutes passed. Robert and Suzanna returned to the room to find Jacob sobbing; they had never seen him so distraught. Suzanna rushed to his side and held his head resting her chin on his forehead. Robert walked briskly to the opposite side of the bed and held his son's hand. No words were spoken. No words were necessary.

It was two days after the crash before Jacob was well enough to see Christina. His wounds were healing quickly, and he was desperate to be with her. The nurses urged him to stay in his room for another day or so, but he was insistent upon seeing Christina. He entered her room with an IV stand in tow. She greeted him with a gentle smile, and a tear rolled down her cheek. She had some small cuts and bruises on the side of her face and her chin.

The tears shed over the past several days left dark creases beneath her eyes.

"Jacob, I am so sorry," she said as the tears flowed once more.

He walked briskly to her side wrapping his arms around her the best way he could with all of the tubes and equipment in the way.

Her room had been filled with flowers and prayer cards from their church. Jacob's parents, Christina's mom, and her friend Holly had all taken turns to be with her in the room to keep her company. They knew Jacob would have wanted them there since he couldn't be. It was Holly's turn to be there when Jacob arrived. When she saw him coming, she smiled, "I need to get something to eat. Jacob, do mind if I run down to the cafeteria?" she said, knowing that they needed some time alone. Jacob nodded with a look of silent appreciation. Holly grabbed her purse and made her way to the door. "Be back soon, friend," she said softly as she slipped out the door.

"Oh, Chrissy," Jacob said with tears swelling up in his eyes, "I am so sorry. I should have taken a different road or left sooner or.."

"Jacob," Christina interrupted in her soothing but broken voice, "Sweetheart, there wasn't anything you could have done different. This isn't your fault; it was an accident."

He knew she was right, but it was Jacob's nature to take ownership of what happened. He felt like it was his job to protect her and that somehow he had let her down. She never wanted him to feel like that; she just wanted him to hold her. Like countless times before in their relationship, he did just that. He held her tight. She always felt better in his arms; that day was no exception. Together they embraced for what seemed like hours. There were no words to describe their pain; they wept together in each other's arms, crying tears of sadness for all that they had lost and tears of joy for all that they still had.

Finally, Christina broke the silence, "I'm sorry I didn't tell you sooner; I wanted it to be a surprise."

"I know", Jacob replied. "It's okay; we're going to be okay."

Chapter 25

A week in the hospital seemed like months for Jacob and Christina. Jacob was discharged several days before Christina was released, but he still spent all of his time by her side. His wounds healed much faster than hers, but his injuries were less severe. Robert & Suzanna took it upon themselves to purchase the wheelchair that Christina would call home for the rest of her life, and they bought the best one they could afford. Robert spent the last few days of her hospital stay building a ramp over the front steps at their house.

The ride home from the hospital left everyone with mixed emotions. Their lives were changed forever. They all felt the despair of loss.

The first week back home was the hardest. Christina was still very weak and unaccustomed to the confines of a wheelchair. She did her best to hide her frustration and to keep Jacob from hovering over her. She made her way to the window and watched the yellow Carolina Jessamine blooms that had grown on their fence gently sway in the breeze. Her modest little garden was sprouting weeds, and the back yard was in dire need of some attention.

"Jacob, the backyard looks terrible."

"I really don't want to leave you here by yourself," he replied.

"I'll be fine. I need to start doing things on my own."

She was right. He didn't like it, but she was right.

"Alright," Jacob relented, "but I'll have my phone with me, so you call me if you need anything. I'll use the bush hog so it shouldn't take too long. If you need anything at all..."

"I will. Now go and get to work." Her playful banter brought a smile to his face. He wanted to stay at her side, but he knew that he couldn't win this particular battle.

Against his better judgment, Jacob walked out the back door towards the barn. It was a dilapidated old building in dire need of repair and a fresh coat of paint. It was about half the size of their little farmhouse but served its purpose in storing all of the tools and equipment they needed to keep their small farm running smooth. As he walked, Jacob stared glassy-eyed and completely zoned out. He was still somewhat in shock and disbelief about the events of the past two weeks.

He reached the large door in front of the barn and committed to himself that it was time to move on with life and return to some semblance of normal. He propped the barn doors open and climbed onto the old tractor his dad had given them as a part of their wedding present. Jacob stepped on the clutch and pushed the rusty start button only to hear the antiquated machine groan.

Still a bit disengaged, Jacob got down from the tractor and made his way over to an old toolbox that sat on his small workbench. After a few minutes mumbling to himself and finding a wrench, he started working on loosening a few bolts near the engine. Jacob had learned a lot about mechanics working on the old tractor. It had been in his family as long as he could remember, and it seemed like it was breaking down every other week.

Jacob was fairly certain that the battery had finally given out in the colder weather, so he immediately started with disconnecting the battery terminals. The first one came off without much effort, but the second one was not as kind. Jacob pulled on the wrench to get the bolt broken loose when suddenly it gave way, and he smashed his finger on one of the nearby engine brackets. Although it did not cut him, the injury was still quite painful. Jacob stepped back toward the wall of the barn with a groan of disgust and clenched his fists in frustration. He could feel the energy pulsing down his arms and the air mixed with dust and dirt began to swirl around his fists.

In a few seconds, his arms began to ache as if the energy contained within his muscles had to be released. Unable to hold back anymore, Jacob swung at the wall of the barn punching a hole right through it. The air stopped swirling and the dust returned to its normal carefree pattern of dancing through the air.

Jacob's shock was suddenly interrupted by a scream coming from the house. He dropped his wrench and took off out the door.

195

The dirt flew up from behind him as he ran and his work boots were making heavy indents in the ground with every step. His breath looked like smoke coming from his mouth in the cold air. The house was about two hundred yards from the barn, but he made it there in almost no time. He came crashing in the door and stopped at the entrance to the kitchen. Christina had moved far from where he left her. She sat in her wheelchair with a tear on each cheek staring wide-eyed toward the floor. The tears were not tears of pain, but tears of frustration. Her forehead was wrinkled, and her face was flush. She didn't move when he entered, and she didn't say a word.

Jacob followed her focus and realized that she was in a stare down with a large cockroach standing its ground about three feet in front of her. Jacob stood still and silent as the sweat beaded and fell from his forehead.

Christina kept her focus on the defiant bug and sniffled as she spoke.

"I can't even kill a roach."

"If looks could kill, he sure would have been dead by now," Jacob said trying to lighten the atmosphere. His untimely attempt at humor was not well received. Christina's faced softened. She changed her focus and looked up at him with her eyes full of tears.

Jacob's demeanor changed quickly as his heart broke for her. He strategically placed his work boots to overtake her adversary as he walked toward her with compassion in his eyes. The crunch of the tiny brown bug broke the heavy pattern of his boots against the old hard wood floor.

"I'm sorry, Chrissy," he said as he kneeled next to her to embrace. She buried her face in his neck and wrapped her arms around his strong body.

"Close your eyes," Jacob whispered. She instinctively closed her eyes and took a deep breath. She felt his arms of comfort and strength. It meant even more to her now that she felt frail. The consistency of his breath and the warmth of his touch calmed her emotions, and she regained her composure.

"Maybe the yard can wait a few more days," he whispered.

Christina took a deep breath, "maybe just a few."

Chapter 26

Jacob woke the next morning to the sound of thunder and the ring of the telephone. He watched Christina for just a second or two. She was flat on her back with her eyes still closed and mouth slightly open. He loved watching her sleep. Just after the third ring, Jacob rolled over and grabbed the phone.

"Hello."

"Good morning, son." The voice was light and familiar.

"Hi mom."

"Did I wake you?"

"Umm…no mom, we were just getting up."

"You have never been a good liar, Jacob Monroe."

Jacob grinned. He felt the warm of Christina's hand on his shoulder.

"Yeah, that's a shame," Jacob retorted. "I would probably get away with more if I was."

"Your dad has been bugging me about making a roast for dinner with all the fixings. I've had the crock pot going all night, and we're going to need someone to come over to the house after church to help us eat all this food."

"Well, I think you can count on us," Jacob replied after getting a smile and approval nod from Christina. "See you soon, mom."

Jacob made every attempt to convince Christina to wear something comfortable to church, but she wouldn't have it. She plainly aired her frustration about dressing and feeling frumpy since the accident, and she was determined to look nice for the day. Not surprisingly, Jacob was not skilled at the art of women's clothing and as a result was more of a hindrance than a help in getting his wife dressed. Still, he did his best and Christina was at his mercy.

The weather was not very accommodating to Christina's desire to look perfect. From the time they had laid down the night before to the time church was over, it had rained steadily.

Despite the weather, Christina was happy to see some of her friends in a normal setting. Most of the people were very genuine and cordial though she did notice a few stares of pity throughout the church service. Jacob didn't leave her side the entire time. Their usual habit of holding hands during the church service meant more to her now. It was not just the touch of her soul mate, it was the touch of her guardian.

Jacob's attempt to make Christina feel comfortable and normal again was extremely successful. They left the church and drove to Robert and Suzanna's house for lunch where the pleasant aroma of southern country cooking met them at the front door. The Monroe's house was quaintly decorated in country style with faded hardwood floors, wallpaper walls, and a classic red plaid tablecloth.

"Looks like some of my prayers were answered," Jacob said as the old truck approached the driveway. Christina glanced over to see him looking at the sky which had finally broken with a ray of sunshine.

"Do you ever wonder if some prayers are easier to answer than others?" she said without thinking. Jacob was silent. He had no response to her question. Christina closed her eyes and tilted her head back with a sigh.

"I'm sorry Jacob. That was stupid. I promised myself that I was going to stop wallowing in self-pity, and then I go and say something like that. Let's rewind the conversation a few minutes and pretend that didn't happen."

Jacob was relieved at her suggestion and happily complied. He parked as close to the front door as possible and gently lifted Christina out of the car and into her wheelchair.

The Monroe's sat down at the table and enjoyed a southern style feast complete with fresh vegetables and Suzanna's famous homemade gravy. The conversation was pleasant but shallow until Jacob said something that struck a chord with his parents.

"What did you say?" Robert asked with a perplexed but concerned look on his face. Suzanna lowered her fork to her plate as her eyes enlarged, and she looked at Robert.

"What?" Jacob asked startled at their response. "I was just saying that I need to get a new battery for the tractor."

"No son, about your hand, what happened?"

"The wrench broke loose, and I slammed my hand into the motor bracket..."

"After that."

"It hurt so much, I hit the wall. The boards must be rotting cause my hand went right through, but don't worry, it's not a big hole. I will fix it as soon as possible." Jacob was starting to feel guilty as though he had broken something that didn't belong to him and was confessing his mistake.

Robert maintained his composure and gave Suzanna a reassuring look. Jacob, still nervous about their response to his story took a quick drink of water and wiped his mouth with his napkin.

"What's going on? Why are you guys acting like this is a big deal?"

"Son, I need your help with something if you don't mind," Robert said calmly.

"Sure."

"We had to take the truck to church this morning. With all the rain, your mom's car got stuck in the mud."

"Umm, yeah, no problem."

Robert slid his chair back and started to rise.

"Wait, Dad...you want to do that right now?"

"It would make me feel better. I've got an old pair of work boots you can borrow, so you don't get your church shoes muddy."

"Ok," Jacob said still confused about the sudden change of environment, "I've got some chain in the truck."

"Don't think we're going to need that," Robert said getting up from his seat. "It just needs a good push."

Both men excused themselves from the table. Christina stayed silent as she and Suzanna watched the men walk out the front door.

"Mom, you want to tell me what that was about?"

"Probably nothing, dear," Suzanna said, though she didn't believe her own words. They had lived such normal lives for so long without thinking about it. When the accident happened, they were both so focused on Christina and Jacob's condition that the restrainer chip didn't even cross their mind. Quick flashbacks of Julie and Jacob when they were little filled her head as she tried to mask her emotions on her face. She stood from her seat and began clearing the table knowing that Christina wasn't going to let it go.

"Mom?"

It was no use. Hearing that word in a soft, feminine, concerning tone was too much for Suzanna. Her mind quickly imagined her lost daughter, grown and beautiful addressing her in the same fashion. She stopped in her tracks and the tears welled up in her eyes. She turned to Christina and said, "I'm sorry, honey.

203

There's something we need to talk to you and Jacob about, but we need to wait until they come back inside."

"Ok," Christina replied, still perplexed but uncomfortable with pressing the issue.

Jacob and Robert walked down the moist but hardened dirt driveway toward Suzanna's oversized Buick sitting just off into the grass enough to have the tires sunk down in the muddy ground. As the men approached the partially buried car, Jacob tried to move past the awkward moment that started at the dinner table and had followed them out to the front yard.

"Dad, I really think this is going to take a tow chain. Anyway, why did she park out here?"

"Your mom had some friends over yesterday from her book club, and she didn't want any of them to feel like they needed to park in the grass, so she moved her car off the driveway. You would think an old farmer's wife would have a better handle on the weather."

Jacob smiled. He could tell that his dad was still trying to hide something from him. Something about the situation felt like a set up, but he played along nonetheless.

"I'll put it in neutral while you push from the back," Robert said.

Jacob was convinced that he would need to resort to the tow chain, but he didn't see much sense in arguing with his dad about it. He would try it Robert's way first and then get to say "I told you so" when the original plan failed. At his dad's request, Jacob walked to the back of the car placing his hands on the rear bumper. His feet sank a bit in the slick mud. Robert sat down in the driver's seat and shifted the transmission into neutral.

"Give it a push, Jacob."

"Ok, dad," Jacob said with a smile knowing that the car wasn't going to budge. He bent over, placed his hands on the rear bumper, and gave it a small nudge.

"Yeah, Dad, we really need to get the tow chain. This beast isn't going anywhere."

"You didn't even try, son. You can give me more than that."

Clearly Robert wasn't going to be convinced until Jacob ruined his church pants by burying them up to the knees in the mud. He dug his feet in the mushy ground and his hands cupped the rear bumper as he filled his muscles with tension. Much to his surprise, the car moved. It moved slowly at first, but then picked up speed. Without looking up, Jacob kept pushing. It felt more like a sled than a car as he took step after step. When he was convinced the vehicle was back on the hardened dirt of the driveway, Jacob stopped pushing and looked up. Deep ruts remained in the ground marking the travel path of the car. Between the ruts were the heavy footprints of muddy work boots. When Jacob looked up from the ruts, he also saw the brake lights and realized that his dad had his foot on the brake the entire time.

"Dad...what's going on?"

"For years, your mom and I worried about a day like this. Let's go back inside. We have to talk to y'all, and we have a phone call to make first thing tomorrow morning."

"Who do we need to call?"

"Tom Marshall."

Chapter 27

Tom Marshall Monitor Log Personal File AMAT715

My workday started at 7:00am this morning. I logged on to my computer and was focused on searching news databases when George walked in.

"Good morning, Tom."

"Morning, George."

The fact that George remained so calm and collected through all this made me very frustrated. We have been back in our Atlanta home base for some time, and it had been nine weeks since our last lead. Richard had simply dropped off the map. The bank robbery in Charlotte offered enough cash for him to stay hidden for a while, but I knew he couldn't stay hidden forever. I also suspected that he was too smart not to be planning something big.

George was the only cheerful person in the building. The weeks of silence had invoked a solemn environment of hopelessness and defeat. The General checked in every day but was hardly ever around which made me feel a little more at ease. There seemed to always be at least one of his men lurking around though. I was certain that their job was to alert the General if we stumbled across a clue, but I never confronted them on it. The General was paranoid that he might get left out of the action. Personally, I was content with his absence.

Every day I followed the same routine, and every day my searching came up empty. The task was becoming mundane, and I felt it was my duty to share my frustration with George the next time he walked by my office.

I waited and watched. George would show up when I was busy chasing a dead-end lead, but now that I needed to vent, he was mysteriously preoccupied. After a few minutes, I decided to pay him a visit in his office.

"George, what are we doing?" I asked as I walked in uninvited and sat in the chair across from his desk.

"What do you mean, Tom?"

"We're doing the same thing every day, and we haven't had a solid lead to follow in weeks."

"Ah, but today is Monday."

"So.... it's the first day of another pointless week."

"No, it's the first day of a week of opportunity, Tom."

"You're killing me, George."

"You propose that we should be doing something else?"

"Yes."

"Like what?"

"I...I don't know." I slumped down in my chair. George had somehow diffused the frustration bomb that I walked into the room with. I didn't have an answer to that question. I suppose my plan wasn't well thought out. Maybe I just needed to hear it said. There wasn't anything more to do. We just needed to keep searching until we found something that would lead us to Richard. I let out a sigh that sounded more like a grunt.

"Uh. This is consuming me."

"That has been your problem since day one, Tom. You let this job consume you, rule your life. There are more things to live for, better things."

"Whoa. You can stop right there, George. I didn't come here for a sermon."

"Of course not, Tom. You are much too stubborn for that. What did you come here for?"

I couldn't answer that question either. I suppose that was strike two for me. At that point, I opted to cut my losses and jump back into the data search that had become my daily routine. I gave George a sarcastic look as I stood and started for the door. Just before I reached the hallway, my phone rang.

"Hello, this is Tom."

"Hello Mr. Marshall, this is Robert Monroe."

The name and the voice stopped me in my tracks. The change in my facial expression caught George's attention, and he leaned forward at his desk waiting for the next few words to come out of my mouth.

"Good morning, Mr. Monroe."

I glanced back at George. By the look on his face, he was just a surprised as I was. He quickly walked around his desk and stood by my side in hopes of hearing both sides of the conversation.

"Good morning, Tom. It has been a long time since we talked."

"Yes, it has. Is everything alright?"

"I suppose I wouldn't be calling if it was." Robert's voice was slow and calm, but he usually didn't waste words. I stepped backwards into George's office and closed the door. George kept right in step with me and stayed close. I could tell Robert wanted to get straight to his point, so I paused and let him continue.

"A couple of weeks ago, Jacob and Christina were in a really bad car accident."

"I am sorry to hear that. Are they okay?"

"I'm afraid not, Tom. The accident damaged Christina's spine and the doctors say that she'll never be able to walk again."

Robert choked up a bit on the last sentence. It was still difficult for him to say without emotion.

"That's terrible, Mr. Monroe. I am so sorry."

"Jacob was hurt in the wreck, but he's okay. At least we thought he was. He has been showing signs of unusual strength, and we're afraid his implant might be damaged."

"Have you told Jacob about his condition?"

"Yes, we talked to both of them yesterday. We told them the truth about Julie and the arrangement we had with you to protect Jacob. It was very hard to explain, but I think they understand. We don't know what to do. They have already lost so much and we're afraid that..."

"Listen, Mr. Monroe, I don't think there's anything to worry about just yet. However, just for the sake of protocol we would like to come down and see both you and Jacob today."

"Yes, of course. Jacob has time off for the holidays, and we can meet you here at our house."

"Great. George and I will be there soon."

As I ended the call, I stared at George waiting for his perspective. The expression on his face was blank. Although he didn't talk excessively, George was rarely at a loss for words. This call rattled him. His blank expression was interrupted by a knock on the door. I opened the door to find Jackson standing at attention on the other side. I was starting to become paranoid that the General had bugged the entire office complex. After an awkward pause, George regained enough composure to break the silence.

"Mr. Jackson, I am glad you came by. Have you or your men picked up any leads?"

"No sir."

"Neither have we, but don't lose heart son, we will catch up to him. Tom and I need to run out for a bit. It's not mission related, but it is important. We will be back this evening. Please call us if you hear of anything."

"Yes sir."

Jackson had a skeptical look on his face as he turned to walk away. He didn't want to believe George, but he had no reason not to. George had stored up a lot of credibility points with the team, which made it hard for anyone to question his words. We both grabbed our jackets and left casually and quietly so to not arouse any more suspicion.

Chapter 28

The car ride felt much longer than it had felt during past visits. George and I had a brief philosophical discussion about why these events were happening now after so many years of silence. We concluded that we were statistically due for an event. George recounted the story of his hometown in north Texas being devastated by two tornados just months apart after three years of calm normal weather. The correlation wasn't quite clear, but I pretended to be interested until he gave up trying to parallel the situations.

It had been well over a year since I visited the Monroe's. Robert and Suzanna were one of the few couples who knew about the monitor department and the restrainer chip. After losing their daughter, they were more than accommodating to our needs. George was their originally assigned monitor in the early years, but as we took on more clients, George transitioned the Monroe family to me. Robert had agreed with me several years ago to contact me if anything suspicious ever happened. I made it a point to keep him updated with my latest phone number, address, and any other contact information just in case.

Our agreement made it easier for me to keep tabs on my other clients, and I only checked in with the Monroe's on rare occasions. They likely didn't even know that the department was shut down months ago. I doubt anyone ever contacted them to tell them. With all the stress of the situation and heightened emotions, I never even thought of letting them know.

Robert was a man of his word. He probably didn't know that I wasn't officially a monitor anymore, but he did know that something had changed in Jacob. He knew that he made a commitment, and his concern for the well-being of his only son offered enough motivation for him to call my cell number.

The Monroe's house was just as I remembered it. A quaint little southern brick farmhouse with battered shutters and a large front porch. The driveway was hard Georgia clay that stretched from the road and rounded off right in front of the house. Robert had built a small ramp to cover the front two steps that was just wide enough for Christina's wheelchair.

Staying true to southern hospitality rules of etiquette, Suzanna walked out the front door of the house before I got both feet out of the car. Her smile was warm and inviting, but her eyes clearly communicated some anxiety.

"Good afternoon, gentlemen," she said.

"Hello, Mrs. Monroe," George responded with a grin.

"Now, George, we dismissed the formalities a long time ago; please call me Suzanna."

She stood at the steps of the porch with arms open. Her warm personality was not going to let either of us pass without a brief hug for a greeting. I appreciated the gesture but couldn't stop myself from getting straight to business.

"Mrs. Monroe.... Suzanna, Robert sounded worried on the phone this morning, so I would like to..."

"Please, Tom, come in and sit down for a bit," Suzanna interrupted unwilling to let me accelerate the traditional order of greeting that had become her habit. "We've been expecting you. Robert, Jacob, and Christina are all in the living room waiting to talk to you both. I've got sweet tea and lemonade in the kitchen, and a fresh batch of cookies that just came out of the oven."

The very words made my stomach growl. I smiled politely and kept quiet until we made our way into the living room. Robert and Jacob both stood as we entered and shook our hands. Although I already felt like I knew Jacob and Christina, they were not as aware of me as I was of them. Jacob politely introduced himself and his wife to me. They had left two open chairs in the room for us, and Suzanna rushed off to the kitchen to retrieve the cookies and drinks.

"Good to see you both again," Robert said as we sat.

"It's good to see you too, "George replied. "Though I wish it were under better circumstances."

As quickly as she had left the room, Suzanna returned with a tray full of snacks and drinks. Being the grateful guest, I accepted the snack. The taste of her cookies and the sweetness of the tea made me wonder why I didn't visit more often. Jacob and Christina sat next to each other with their hands intertwined. Beyond the hospitable greeting, they stayed silent as if still stunned by the news of Jacob's condition. The air was thick with unanswered questions until Robert broke the silence.

"Tom, we think something has happened to Jacob's restrainer chip in the car accident. We didn't connect the dots at first, but after the wreck, Jacob healed quickly and has become stronger than ever. We are concerned that his chip is broken and, quite honestly, we are afraid of what might happen to him if we don't get things checked out in a timely manner."

My initial rush to get straight to business subsided as I fell under the calming influence of the homemade sweet tea. I took a quick sip and responded in a much more casual but professional manner.

"I understand your concerns, Mr. Monroe. Jacob, I am sorry we had to keep secrets from you, but you must know that it was in your best interest."

Jacob nodded, "Dad and I had a long talk about it, and I understand. As you can see, the accident had a big impact on our family and our lives. My only interest now is to make sure I can continue to take care of my wife." As he spoke, Jacob glanced down at Christina, not with a look of pity but one of compassion. "We've been through a lot together, and I'll do whatever it takes to stay with her."

George responded in a deep, crackled voice. "I understand, Jacob. Don't worry. We have procedures to handle situations like this, and we can get you set up with a new chip in no time. Our mission has always been to give you and others like you the opportunity for a normal, happy life. I don't believe you are in any immediate danger, but even so, we will get you scheduled for a chip re-implant as soon as possible." George's voice was calming and convincing. The heaviness of the air in the room almost lifted completely until I jumped in the conversation with a shocking proposal.

"Jacob," I said, "before you get a new chip implant, I would like you to consider something." George turned to me with an unusual stare that combined surprise with uncertainty. I continued.

"You aren't the first one to have a chip malfunction. In fact, there's a young man who has similar abilities as yours. His chip was also damaged not long ago. He has done some really bad things and is hiding from us right now. We really could use your help in bringing him under control once we track him down."

Everyone shared a look of bewilderment. Out of the corner of my eye I could see George's look of horror. Robert opened his mouth as if to say something before Jacob interrupted him.

"Mr. Marshall, I am sorry about your situation, but I can't help you. Right now we just need to focus on getting ourselves back to a healthy normal."

"Of course, of course," George said trying to dismiss my request as quickly as possible. "We can get you scheduled in to see a surgeon early next week. We'll get you checked out to identify the problem and ensure we pursue the right fix. In the meantime, please be careful with everything you handle and try to resume normal life as much as possible."

"We will, Mr. Miller. Please call us as soon as you can with the details for the procedure," Jacob said as he stood with his arm outstretched toward George. Robert, George, and I all stood and shook hands before Suzanna popped back in from the kitchen to escort us back to the front porch.

"We will," George replied. "It was very good to see all of you again. Thank you for your hospitality, and we will be in touch."

"Thank you again Suzanna for the treats," I said as I grabbed a cookie for the road. She smiled and led us to the front door.

"Thank you for coming over. Please stay in touch," she said as we passed her and walked down the front steps, "and drive safe."

George beat me to the driver's side of the car and as he sat down put his hand out for the keys. His pleasant demeanor became a look of disapproval as soon as we pulled out of the driveway. I had seen that look in him before, and I knew I was in for a lecture.

"We are supposed to protect the elite, not exploit them."

"Oh, come on, George. You can't tell me the thought didn't cross your mind. The timing was perfect. Jacob's chip malfunctions right at the time we could use his ability to bring Richard under control. Destiny gave us an opportunity, and you're upset at me for asking the question?"

"You know that's not part of the job."

"You know Jacob's profile as well as I do. He's a good guy with a bit of a hero complex, and he is categorized as a Class 3 just like Richard. He could really..."

"That's enough, Tom. We're not going there. Jacob is being the hero he needs to be by taking care of his family. It's not his job to get this mess cleaned up. It's ours. Whatever ideas you had about a grand battle of the titans needs to be abandoned right now. We are going to follow protocol, deal with Richard, and then get on with life. Am I clear?"

"Yes, sir."

George was being narrow-minded, and I had not seen him that upset in years. I knew arguing with him wasn't going to change his position, so I dropped the topic altogether. A deafening silence filled the car the rest of the way back to our home base. It was late when we arrived, and George forced himself to offer me a polite but short goodbye before he stepped out of the car and walked away gracefully.

Tom Marshall Monitor Log Personal File AMAT715

End of Record

Chapter 29

Tom could tell that George was still a bit irritated with him the next morning. George's normal cheerful appearance was replaced with a stoic but polite greeting as he walked in the office. The leftover tension between George and Tom was evident, but there was also an atmosphere of apprehension in the building and neither of them knew why. It felt like something bad was going to happen, but no one knew what it was.

The General and many of his men were gone, leaving the offices vacant and still. It was odd for them not to have a presence this early in the morning. Tom's intuition quickly became reality as he booted up his computer to begin checking for recent news events that could lead to their illusive target.

The hottest news story of the day had ignited just thirty minutes before Tom got to his office, and it was the topic of every major news channel. Unfortunately, it was a scene that was all too familiar in our nation, and it was unfolding just over an hour away at the University of Georgia campus in Athens. The event began with a massive explosion at the University School of Law and authorities had cornered a lone gunman in the library.

Fortunately, most of the student body was gone for the holidays but there were still several students and faculty in the area preparing for the next semester.

Tom immediately pulled up all the news channels and had several vantage points showing on his computer screens. George instantly put aside the tension between them and briskly walked in with a deep look of concern on his face.

"Are you seeing this, Tom?"

"Yea. I've got three of the news cameras on the scene pulled up now."

"What do we know?"

"Looks like a lone terrorist. They're guessing he's part of some anti-government group that recently developed on campus. No confirmation yet on any casualties, but there was an explosion in one of the buildings and now they have him held up in the library with hostages."

"Do we know how many hostages?"

"Not that anyone is reporting. He is definitely armed though, and I am guessing by what they've shown so far that it is some high dollar firepower."

George didn't respond. They were both shaken by the event as they sat silently scanning all three screens streaming live coverage. Police cars and military vehicles surrounded the front of the library with more than fifty men poised and ready to shoot. The news cameras were fixed on the library entrance while reporters rambled to fill the tense moments. Ten minutes passed and the stalemate continued. Another fifteen minutes passed, and nothing happened. Everyone was waiting for the next move.

Tom and George watched expecting to see the gunman come out and surrender or take his own life. Enough time had passed for a hostage negotiator to be sent in. These scenarios were all part of similar incidents in the recent past, but this one played out much differently.

Instead of seeing one man coming out of the library, they saw one heading toward the library. He crossed the police line and despite the harsh orders from the police to stop, he kept walking. As the man drew the attention of the news cameras, George and Tom both squinted to see the grainy image of the man. They gasped simultaneously at the unexpected sight.

"Tom, pull that news feed up on our secure server," George said as he rushed out of the office. It had been a long time since George moved that fast. He wasn't gone for more than thirty seconds before the public news video went black. The news reporters tried to excuse the black out as a technical failure, but Tom knew that George had made some higher-level phone calls to blind the rest of the world from this event. Cameras were still rolling on the scene and feeding directly into their system and only their system. George scurried back into Tom's office.

"Are we sure it's him?"

"No doubt George, it's Richard."

Tom was torn between wanting to keep his gaze fixed on the computer screen and wanting to abandon it to drive to the campus knowing that he would never make it there in time. They both sat on the edge of their seats with a private viewing of what was quickly becoming more than just an average school shooting.

"What do you think he's doing, Tom?" George said without moving his eyes off the screen.

"Richard is a smart guy. I'm not sure what his motive is, but I think we are about to find out."

As Richard moved closer, suddenly two gun shots rang out from the library entrance. The cameraman flinched and moved to a safer location behind his news van not realizing that George and Tom were the only ones seeing his camera shot.

As the camera steadied from the movement, they could see Richard on the ground flat on his back. He was only there for a few seconds before he sat up and got back on his feet. He took three more steps toward the entrance and another gunshot pierced the air. Richard's left shoulder drew back affecting his balance, but it didn't knock him down.

When he was approximately twenty feet from the steps at the entrance to the library, Richard sprinted past the pillars and burst through the glass door. Four more gun shots were heard. The momentary silence was broken by a dark clothed body hurled through the front window. Richard strutted back through the broken front door and stood over the man who was lying on his side on the front lawn. He then looked straight toward the news camera as if to address an audience.

"My name is Richard Hall. I have the power and ability to help a lot of people, but I am being chased by government officials who..."

Richard's speech was interrupted by the presence of an exploding gas can just inches away from his feet. The white cloud of gas spewed all around him as armed military troops ran with guns drawn toward Richard. As the camera panned right, Tom saw General Corbin on the sideline calling the shots.

Richard darted from the white cloud coughing and ran around to the right side of the library building with masked military men in pursuit. Several of the men stopped with guns poised at the young man still lying on the ground who was choking on the gas and wounded from the ordeal.

Richard clearly had an escape route planned out. His strategy served him well as he dashed out of sight. The gun shots continued to ring out as he ran, and several military jeeps joined in the pursuit. He zipped past the School of Law building that was still smoking from the explosion. The jeeps were driving full speed over grass, shrubs, and walkways as gunfire continued to fly.

Richard crossed Lumpkin Street and continued to swerve and dodge past the campus buildings and dormitory areas, slowly creating some distance between himself and his pursuers. The

Generals' men did their best to keep up but didn't have much of a chance.

Tom lost the live camera footage just after Richard darted away from the gas cloud, so he and George immediately called in a ten-mile perimeter with the local authorities and rushed to the scene as soon as they could.

Richard's speed and agility proved to be more than the General's determination as he continued to run west. The back of his shirt was marked with bullet hits, but his adrenaline was flowing so heavily that it didn't even phase him.

His exit route was planned and coordinated so that his ability gave him the advantage he needed to escape. Once more, Richard slipped past the team and disappeared. Although he knew that he didn't get his entire message out to the world, he was hoping that his act of staged heroism was enough to convince the public that he was the good guy. He was convinced that if he could win the public opinion, he could erase a lot of the sin of his recent past. His marketing plan was genius, and it almost worked.

Richard was anxious to find a place where he could witness his performance on the news. After creating quite a bit of distance between himself and the search party, he found a local restaurant with televisions mounted throughout the interior. He was increasingly frustrated to discover that the news feeds had been severed, and his performance went unnoticed by the public's attention.

George and Tom knew that they did the right thing by stifling Richard's media appeal to society, but they also knew that their actions would amplify his frustration and desperation. The situation had become a dangerous strategy game with a significant amount of uncontrollable power at stake. In order to outsmart Richard, Tom knew that he needed some advantage. It had become time to step up his game and bend some of his own integrity rules. He was willing to do whatever it took to get connected with Richard, and the next step was getting some time with a young man wearing a black overcoat who had some firsthand experience with Richard's capabilities.

Chapter 30

Michael Ray Dobson was a young and disturbed college student. His pale white skin, jet black short hair, and thin frame made him look younger than he really was. Michael's dad dropped out of his life when he was just a baby, and his mom struggled to make ends meet as a tattoo artist. She cycled through boyfriends regularly but usually attracted the same type of abusive relationship. Michael found some level of belonging with the gothic crowd and quickly assimilated himself to that particular look complete with eyebrow piercings and dark eye makeup.

Michael's mom was in the middle of a legal battle with the Internal Revenue department regarding a tax evasion issue. The situation resulted in their eviction from the small apartment they called home and meant that Michael was going to lose his government financial assistance at the end of this semester.

At nineteen years old, Michael had been duped into playing the role of college campus terrorist in a scheme devised by someone who knew how to appeal to people's wants and needs. Stripped of his dark black wardrobe, Michael lay in a secure hospital room at Athens Regional Medical Center. Armed military guards stood watch outside his door only allowing access to specific doctors, George, and Tom. The General had done a fair job of locking down the situation, though Tom would never verbally compliment him on it.

George and Tom arrived at the medical center just after the doctors had completed their initial evaluation. By the time they arrived, the General had already left to join the field search for Richard. Jackson escorted them to see Doctor Murray.

"He sustained a few cracked ribs and is pretty bruised up but no major injuries," Doctor Murray said as he kept his focus on his clipboard.

"Thank you, Doctor," George replied is his traditional kind demeanor.

George and Tom both entered the room to see Michael lying in bed sedated and eyes bloodshot red from the gas. He stared out the window and didn't acknowledge their entrance. George pulled up a nearby chair next to his bedside while Tom propped himself up next to the window.

"Good morning, Michael. My name is George, and I would like to talk to you about what's been going on the past few weeks."

Michael didn't respond.

"You're going to need to trust me, Michael. We can help you if you will just…"

"Stop calling me that. I have nothing to say to you so go away."

George paused, leaned back in his chair for a moment and then stood. He slowly moved the chair back where he found it and turned to leave.

"If you change your mind, please let me know," George said as he walked to the door. George glanced at Tom for a moment as he walked out the door, but Tom didn't move. Tom recognized this as his only chance to get some information without George questioning his tactics. After pausing long enough for George to be out of earshot, Tom addressed Michael.

"What do you want to be called?" Tom said in a serious tone. Michael paused never shifting his eyes away from the window.

"Dagger," he mumbled, "my name is Dagger."

Tom moved closer to his bedside and lowered his voice to a whisper.

"Ok Dagger, here's the deal. I think we both know that you're in a lot of trouble, and I don't think this is all your fault. I have a lot of influence in deciding what happens to you next and can make things a lot easier if you can tell me what you know about Richard Hall."

The name caught Michael's attention. His demeanor changed from one of apathy to one suppressing emotion and his eyes focused on Tom. Dagger felt betrayed by Richard, and Tom had struck a nerve.

"I don't trust your friend," Michael said with a piercing stare.

"I don't trust him either," Tom said playing along, "George's interests here are different than mine. I am interested in catching up to Richard. Nothing more, nothing less."

"He's a liar. He told me that we would show them." His face hardened as if it suddenly became stone.

There were clearly some anger issues at hand with Michael. From the short amount of research Tom could do on the way to the crime scene, he knew that Michael was a kid ripe with problems.

"Listen Dagger, Richard is going to pay for what he's done. He's the one who got you into this mess, and he needs to feel the pain. If you know anything about where I can find him, I can make this better."

"Can you tell the cops this wasn't my fault?"

"Absolutely."

"Can you get the feds off my Mom's back?"

"I can."

"Can you get my college money back?"

"I will, Dagger, you have my word."

Tom's confidence made him believable enough for Dagger to open up. His voice was soft and squeaky. Dagger told Tom how he had met Richard at the University. After he and his mom were evicted from their apartment, she went to live with her boyfriend, and Richard let Dagger stay at his place when things at home got rough. From there, he started rambling about the plan and how hey were going to show everyone what real power looked like. Tom did his best to piece together the story as he mumbled hrough it. Richard was a smooth talker and had used his skills to win Dagger's trust. After he inserted himself in Dagger's world, he manipulated him, stirred his unstable emotions, and devised the terror scheme as a part of the government revolution they planned together. The whole plan was a scam so that Richard could keep his own agenda hidden, and Dagger became a pawn in Richard's game.

"Is he still there?" Tom asked.

"I don't know. It's over on State Street. Near the car dealership."

"Thanks, Dagger," Tom said as he turned toward the door. Michael resumed his hardened expression and again faced the window with a blank stare.

Tom walked out of the room and down the hall to meet George who was standing near the elevator waiting in anticipation.

"Tom, did he say anything to you?"

"No. I tried everything possible; he wouldn't say anything."

Chapter 31

Tom Marshall Monitor Log Personal File AAMS35

George and I joined the field search for Richard, but he didn't leave many clues behind. After lying to Michael and to George, I decided to wait until evening to make my move so I wouldn't arouse suspicion. The perimeter search expanded each hour and by five o'clock the teams were so spread out that the chances of finding Richard were slim. I told George that I was going to run out for a bite to eat and headed for my car.

The sun was breaking through the tree line as I arrived at the apartment complex on State Street. It was much more run-down than Richard was accustomed to, but I'm guessing that it was one of those places where you could pay rent in cash on a weekly basis without a lot of questions. I parked on the curb behind a moving truck next to the walkway that was in front of the apartment where Michael said Richard had been staying. The blinds were closed, but I could tell that a light was on inside.

Armed with only a Taser and my wits, I walked slowly toward the front door. I peered in the window through a gap in the blinds, but I didn't see any movement. I knocked on the door and listened. I waited and watched for movement in the room, but there was no response. Richard might have expected Michael to spill everything he knew after Richard tricked and betrayed him. He may have moved on already. Even if he was still naïve enough to stay here, it was clear that he wasn't there at the moment.

Disappointed, I walked back to my car. As I walked past the back of the moving truck, I was startled by the rear door opening. Before I could react, an arm reached out, grabbed me by the back of my collar and slung me across the inside of the truck. The Taser flew out of my pocket on onto the ground outside the truck. I hit the inside wall of the truck hard and fell to the floor as the door closed again.

"I was expecting you sooner," the voice in the dark said, "what took you so long?"

I recognized the voice. It was Richard. My eyes were still adjusting to the darkness. The only light that penetrated the compartment were the small holes in the side and back of the truck where Richard had been keeping an eye out for visitors. The smell inside the truck was a clear indicator that he had been waiting for a long time. He moved closer to me.

"Who are you?" he said in a dark, angry tone.

Any situation I previously thought was dangerous paled in comparison to this. I was trapped by a desperate man; a man that could

236

ill me with his bare hands. My breath was short and my heart was acing. It felt like there wasn't enough air in the room. There was no vay out. The only exit was blocked by Richard who wasn't going to let me go until he got answers.

"Why are you chasing me? How did you stop the news footage? What do you want from me?"

As he screamed the last question, he winced and grunted from the sharp pain that filled his head. My mind was filled with sporadic thoughts. I remembered the confrontation at Camp Pennington, what Jennifer had told us about Richard and the bank in Charlotte. I tried to focus my thoughts and calm him down.

"Richard, this isn't your fault. I want to help you."

"By shooting at me or shocking me?" Richard asked, "I don't believe you. You're hunting me like a wild animal. Did you do this to me?" There was an awkward silence as Richard began to stand straight from his bent position and continued his interrogation. "You were there at the kid's camp, and you were there in Charlotte. Who are you, and what do you want?"

My thoughts were giving me away. I had to calm down and focus, but my body was trembling.

"Ok...ok," I replied, still cowering in fear. The pain Richard was enduring trying to extract my thoughts left him cringing next to the side of the truck. He had one hand on his head and one hand on the wall of the truck propping himself up. My eyes finally adjusted to the darkness, and I could see his anger. He refused to look at me. He wanted to extract the answers from my head, but that had proven too painful. He needed to resort to the threat of physical violence, and honestly, that was enough for me. I kept my eyes focused on the floor and I spoke. I started with a brief history of the elite and the need for the monitoring department. I told him about the restrainer chip and how he could stop the headaches.

I expected Richard to trust me and accompany me back to headquarters so we could end this diplomatically. My hopes were dashed as he grabbed me by the shirt and pinned me against the side wall of the truck.

"This is your last warning. Stop chasing me."

His grip was so tight that I could not respond. He was pressing so hard against my chest that I couldn't inhale. He gave me one last glare and then tossed me against the opposite side of the truck. Everything went black.

I woke up covered in sweat. My chest ached and the pain in my head was piercing. It was too dark for my eyes to focus. I reached up to touch a sensitive knot on the top of my head and kept blinking to try to regain focus. The floor was hard and dirty. I felt around with my hands and concluded that I was still in the back of the moving truck. The air was thick, and the smell was horrible. I stumbled toward the

238

back of the truck using my hands to search for the door. After a few seconds of panicked fumbling, I found the handle and pulled the door up. It raised a few feet and the glow of a streetlight captured my eyes. The rush of fresh air was cold on my brow.

I rolled out of the truck still weak and in pain. As I hopped down, my legs gave way, and I hit the asphalt hard. I looked around to see a very unfamiliar parking lot filled with tractor trailers. Richard had knocked me unconscious, driven me to a truck stop, and abandoned me. I didn't know where I was or what time it was. I only knew that it was nighttime, I was hurting, and my own body odor was making me sick.

Richard had stripped me of my wallet but left me with my phone. He may have been concerned that stealing my phone would give us a way to track him. Whatever the reason, it was the only thing familiar to me, so I was grateful. I checked my location and called George. He answered in a groggy voice.

"Hello?"

"George, its Tom."

"Tom, what's wrong, it's almost midnight."

"I know. I found Richard."

"What? Where?"

"No time for details now. I'm stranded at a truck stop just off Interstate 40 east of Atlanta. I need you to come pick me up."

"What happened, Tom?"

"I'll tell you more when you get here. Right now I need to get home so I can get cleaned up. We need to be prepared to mobilize first thing in the morning."

"Ok, Tom, I'm on my way."

Tom Marshall Monitor Log Personal File AAMS35

End of Record

Chapter 32

"Are you sure you're going to be alright?"

"Yes, Dad, I'll be fine," Christina said as Robert's truck came to a stop on the street in front of the Flint Chemical lab building. The downtown buildings were old and not handicap friendly. Christina was accustomed to parking in the back and coming through the rear door, but the tall steps in the back forced her to come through the front door. She did her best to mask the frustration of her wheelchair and regain as much of a normal life as possible. Robert was kind enough to offer to pick her up from home and take her to work. Christina often thought that she couldn't have asked for better in-laws.

Robert turned off the engine and reached for the door handle when Christina interrupted.

"Dad, I just wanted to say thank you for..." She stopped and closed her eyes to regain her composure.

"Sweetheart, it's really no problem."

Christina looked up and smiled. Robert gently put his arm on her shoulder.

"You know we love you, Chrissy. Now, you better get on in there. You know they can't survive any longer without you."

"I guess I do have some catching up to do," Christina said with a smile.

Robert opened the door and walked toward the back of his truck to get Christina's wheelchair giving her the time to whisper a little prayer before tackling a day at work. This was her first day back at the lab since the accident. She felt she could have taken more time off, but she knew that convincing Jacob to go back to work meant she needed to do the same.

Robert opened the door, looked her right in the eye, and said "My lady, your chariot awaits". It was a corny way to start the day but as much as she thought it was cheesy, she really did enjoy his dry humor. It was obvious that Jacob took after his father. Robert gently lifted Christina out of the truck and placed her gingerly in the wheelchair. She wouldn't let him push her, but she did let him hold the front door for her.

"Do you need anything else?" he asked as she made her way through the door.

"No, I got it from here. Thanks again, Dad."

"See you at four then. Have a great day."

"You too, Dad," she said turning her head to bid him farewell.

The lobby of the building was small with dated wallpaper but still maneuverable for Christina. To the left of the front door there was a small unoccupied reception desk with a single phone. She rolled past the desk toward the door on the right which led to a small hallway. The hallway contained the stair access to the

242

upper level where most of the lab personnel worked, two light fixtures in need of dusting, and a few scenic portraits on the wall. Since the building was old, the hallway wasn't very wide, but it was her only path to the lab where she worked in the back of the building.

The lab staff did everything they could to rearrange obstacles for Christina in preparation for her return. The pathway was manageable but still narrow and sometimes frustrating. The picture that she kept on her desk of herself and Jacob was the first thing she looked at every day when she arrived at her work area. It captured her attention once more and brought a reassuring smile to her face.

"Good morning, Sunshine," Holly said, feeling a bit ignored by her friend and coworker.

"Oh, good morning, Holly. Sorry, I'm in a bit of a fog today."

"Well, you better snap out of it before you process that order for Dr. Johnson today. You know how picky he is, and I'm not cutting you any slack, Monroe." Holly was still a bit uncomfortable with seeing her friend restricted to a wheelchair, and the playful banter helped her deal with the situation. Christina understood and fired right back with her own snappy comment.

"I don't expect you to cut me any slack. Wheels or no wheels, I can still run circles around you, so do your best to keep up."

"Oh, it's on now, hot rod," Holly replied with eyebrows raised and a small grimace on her face.

The first hour went by quickly. Christina always felt the time passed easily as long as there was a backlog of work. At mid morning they heard the door buzzer indicating that someone had come in the front door.

"The delivery guy must be early today," Christina said looking up at Holly.

"Yeah, this would be a first," Holly replied, "I'll get it, hot rod."

Holly walked to the front lobby area. The lab didn't get many visitors throughout the day with the exception of the medical supply deliveries in and out. Most of the staff sat upstairs leaving the visitor relations to Holly and Christina.

As she walked through the door into the lobby, she was stunned to see a handsome and young muscular man standing just inside the front door. His eyes were bloodshot, and his face was slightly scruffy. He wore blue jeans, a plain green t-shirt and a hoodie that casted a shadow on his forehead. His expression was rough, and his eyes looked aggressive as they glanced around the room. His body language made Holly more than a little uncomfortable, and she quickly developed a sinking feeling in her stomach that something just wasn't right.

"Can I help you?" Holly asked.

"I am looking for Christina Monroe."

"And your name?"

"My name is Richard."

Chapter 33

"Just a minute, let me see if she is available. Wait right here," Holly said with a smile as she turned and left back through the door toward the lab. As she got closer to Christina, her paced quickened, and her face revealed the anxiety bubbling from within. She burst through the door to find Christina on the telephone.

"Christina, there is some strange guy here asking for you."

"What?" Christina said looking up at Holly.

"Yeah, something isn't right. I got a really bad feeling when he asked to see you. I played it off though and told him I would see if you are available."

"Is he still out there?" Christina said holding her hand loosely over the phone handset.

"Yeah, what should we do?"

"Holly, it's probably not a big deal. I'll just go out there and see what he wants."

"Umm, I really don't think that's a good idea."

Christina's attention turned back to her phone conversation as the voice on the other end of the line questioned her.

"Chrissy, is everything alright?"

It was Jacob. He was driving to the local machine shop to pick up a part he ordered for a project at work. Anytime he left the plant, he would use the driving time to check up on Christina. His tone sounded just as concerned as Holly's.

"Yes sweetheart, I'm sure it's fine," she said trying to be as reassuring as possible.

"I don't like the sound of it Chrissy. Holly's not the type to overreact."

"Listen, this isn't anything to panic over. It's just a visitor in the lobby. Let me go take care of this real quick, and I'll call you at lunch."

"Please be careful. I love you."

"I love you, too," she said as she hung up the phone. When she looked up, Holly was already gone. Christina began to maneuver her chair around her desk and rolled toward the door.

Holly reentered the lobby area to find the man still standing there with his hands in his jacket pockets. The circles under his eyes seemed darker than before.

"I'm sorry sir, she isn't available right now. If you can leave some contact information, I can have her call you later."

"I'm afraid that's just not acceptable," he said, "I need to see her right now."

"I'm sorry, but…"

Holly stepped back as the man approached her with determination. He brushed her to the side and walked through the

246

doorway toward the lab. Holly rushed toward the reception desk phone. Just as he was halfway down the hallway, Christina's wheelchair appeared from the lab room.

"Can I help you, sir," Christina said in her friendliest southern voice.

"I need to see Christina Monroe."

"I am Christina. What can I do for you?"

"I need some Pretadoxine."

"I'm sorry sir, what did you say?"

"Pretadoxine. I need some now."

"Pretadoxine? What is it for?"

"It's for my headaches. I was told it would fix my headaches."

"I'm not familiar with that drug, sir. Perhaps you should see a doctor. We are just a lab processing facility, but I can give you a recommendation of a doctor in the area and..."

"Don't lie to me Miss Monroe. I know you are developing Pretadoxine here and that you have access to it."

Richard's frustration quickly became anger, and Christina felt a knot in the pit of her stomach. His face turned harsh and the glare of his eyes confirmed Holly's intuition. He slowly walked down the hallway toward her.

"Sir, we don't have that drug here."

"Then you're going to take me where I can get some."

As he reached for her wheelchair a loud alarm resounded through the building. In addition to calling the police, Holly had pulled the fire alarm and triggered an evacuation of the building. Richard grabbed her wheelchair and pulled it in front of him. He pushed it back down the hallway toward the lobby. Several of lab staff came down the stairs right behind Richard. Suddenly Holly appeared from the lobby door and yelled for them to stop the hooded man. The men did their best, but they were no match for Richard's strength and desperation. One of the men was launched back down the hall toward Christina's desk and the other was knocked unconscious on the floor.

Christina tried to break away from Richard, but she couldn't maneuver fast enough down the narrow hallway. With the fire alarm still ringing, Richard regained control of her wheelchair and hurried toward the lobby door. Christina waved her arms frantically for Holly to move out of the way, but she stood her ground.

The impact of the wheelchair forced Holly back through the lobby door and she landed on her side. Richard pushed Christina around her friend and toward the front door. She delayed their exit for a few seconds by grabbing one of the wheels enough to turn the chair and wedge it in the door frame. She fought with her arms to stop him, but she was too weak. He dislodged the wheelchair and pushed it out the front door. She grabbed the wheels to try to stop, but the force created a friction burn on her hands. She quickly let go.

"I don't have what you want," Christina said with tears in her eyes and panic in her voice, "please just let me go."

Just as they exited the front of the building, a police car with lights flashing and siren blazing came down the street toward the cab.

Richard pulled up on the handles of the wheelchair sending Christina plummeting to the ground on the sidewalk near the curb. He hurled the chair at the police car. It smashed the windshield, and sent the vehicle crashing into a row of parked cars across the street. The squealing of tires on the next block over caught Richard's attention. He was expecting to see another police car but instead saw an old pickup truck careening toward him.

Christina was still lying on the curb and peered down the street to see the familiar shape of a pickup truck.

"Jacob," she said exasperated.

Chapter 34

Richard moved out into the center of the street as Jacob's truck came barreling toward him. Jacob could see his wife lying on the curb on the side of the street, and adrenaline coursed through his body. He was determined to protect his wife. He locked his focus on the man who had thrown her to the ground and glared at him with a fire in his eyes as he kept his foot heavy on the gas pedal.

Overconfident in his strength, Richard stepped back with his right foot and raised his fists with every intention of stopping the truck dead in its tracks. Richard never fared well in physics class. Despite his strength, the truck hit him square in the torso sending him flying through the air and landing on the windshield of an oncoming car. The driver slammed on the brakes and the car came to a stop with Richard's body denting the fractured glass. The driver fled on foot leaving the car door wide open. Richard grasped the car door and jerked it from its hinges.

Jacob slammed the brakes, and the old pickup truck came to a screeching halt thirty feet past where Christina lay. He jumped out of the truck and ran toward her. Suddenly he felt a large metal object hit him in the back and knock him to the ground. For only half a second Jacob was dazed. He looked up to see his wife still lying near the street curb with panic and tears in her eyes. To his right the car door that had collided with his back was rocking back and forth on the hard pavement. His back felt bruised, but he didn't see any blood. Jacob stood and turned around to see his attacker running at him full speed. Jacob braced himself and tightened his muscles. He was positioned exactly where he wanted to be – in between Christina and her assailant.

Richard approached quickly and confidently. He was resolute about getting to Christina and the drug that he thought could cure him. Richard kept his running stance in an effort to plow right over Jacob, grab Christina, and get out of the area before he attracted too much more attention. He was shocked when Jacob landed a timely punch just as he advanced. Richard's head jerked back, and he lost his balance. The blow stopped him in his tracks and threw him to the ground. The pain throbbed all over his face. His expression was both surprised and angry. He locked eyes with Jacob, and he scrambled back to his feet.

"Stay away from my wife," Jacob scowled still in a defensive fighting stance. His entire body was tense, and his hand throbbed from the sudden impact with Richard's face.

Richard quickly realized that he wasn't as unique as he thought. Part of him wanted to interrogate Jacob to find out more about what was going on, but the animal instinct in him kept him focused on getting what he wanted and getting out. As he stared at Jacob in bewilderment, the searing pain rose once more in his head. He winced and turned his focus back to Christina.

"Get out of my way," Richard grunted as he once more tried to pass Jacob. This second attempt met with similar results as the first. Jacob grabbed the front of Richard's shirt and hurled him back to the ground next to the mangled car door.

The pain in Richard's head fueled the rage within his body. In one smooth motion, he grabbed the car door, stood to his feet, and swung the blunt object at Jacob. The blow caused Jacob to stumble back toward where Christina was. Jacob was keenly aware of Christina's position. He had lost some ground and had to get some more distance between her and the danger that was bent on hurting her.

Jacob didn't have any fancy fighting style, so he relied purely on instinct. He darted toward Richard and a flying tackle sent both men careening into the side of Jacob's truck. Richard retaliated with a left hook planted squarely on Jacob's jaw. Jacob swung his right fist but was stopped by Richard right hook. Instinctively, Jacob grabbed Richard's other arm, and they were soon locked in a stalemate.

From the small shops and buildings along the downtown street, people appeared to satisfy their curiosity. Many of the town people knew who Jacob was. One man darted out from the small hardware store to break up the street fight but stopped when he heard Jacob yell.

"Stay back," Jacob said gruffly still in a gridlock with Richard.

From the small local bookstore, an elderly lady slowly made her way to Christina's side while keeping her gaze fixed on the action in the middle of the street. She knelt down next to Christina who had propped herself up with her arms and was focused on Jacob. Another man had followed the elderly lady and placed a jacket over Christina who was shivering in the cold. She kept her eyes locked on her husband. She was both desperate and powerless to help him.

Both men grunted as if expelling all their energy at once. Finally, Richard's arm broke Jacob's grip and dealt a blow that jolted his head and sent him to his knees. Jacob attempted an uppercut, but Richard dodged as if he knew it was coming. Richard side-swiped Jacob's legs, and he landed hard on the pavement. Jacob tried to fight back, but Richard dodged every move he made and soon had Jacob pinned to the road. Richard's familiarity with his power gave him a distinct advantage over Jacob who didn't have the time to adapt to these new strength thresholds.

The fight that began as an equally weighted battle of giants quickly became a one-sided thrashing with Jacob on the painful side of the battle. Tears flowed freely from Christina's eyes as she watched from the sideline. In recent weeks she had felt frustrated and confined, but she never felt more helpless than she did in that moment. She watched in horror as Richard landed blow after blow on Jacob's body.

Driven by sheer destitution, Christina closed her eyes and did the only thing she could do. She cried out to God in a passionate plea to save her husband. The words were strong and desperate. She prayed for deliverance, and she prayed for intervention. The elderly lady that had knelt by her side put her feeble little hand on Christina's shoulder and bowed her own head. A few others gathered around Christina and joined in silent prayer while the battle raged on just yards away. Christina felt a hand on her shoulder, and she continued to pray. She felt as though an arm of strength and comfort blanketed her. Suddenly, her mind was clear and an inner-peace calmed her heart. It felt similar to Jacob's arms embracing her, but it was stronger and lighter. Her prayer of desperation soon became a prayer of power. Her expression changed from that of panic to that of determination as a few more people left the crowd of bystanders, closed their eyes, and mouthed their own prayers.

Richard continued to pulverize Jacob's body, countering every strike and avoiding every defense. The battle looked hopeless for Jacob until a sharp pain in Richard's head threw him off his attack rhythm and left him vulnerable to a side punch. The pain was sharp, and Richard dropped his guard to press his hand onto the temple of his head. The pause was enough for Jacob to twist his torso and throw Richard to the side. Richard kept one hand on his head and tried to regain his balance while Jacob stammered to his feet.

Richard's head was full of murmuring. The sound became louder and louder. There seemed to be too many voices in his ears. Each voice was unique but there were too many to focus on one distinguishable sound. He heard a few words from one voice but then that voice was overpowered by another as if hundreds of people were screaming to capture his attention. Each voice he heard magnified the pain in his head. Richard closed his eyes tight, but the voices only intensified.

Jacob stabilized himself against the side of his truck as Richard tried to block out the voices. An elderly female voice was overlaid with a strong masculine voice and a young adolescent voice. The sounds pounded in his head, making him nauseated and unable to focus on restraining Jacob. Suddenly, one voice rose above the others and brought a mental picture to his mind. It was a voice that he had recently heard; it was the sweet but powerful voice of Christina Monroe.

As soon as Richard distinguished the voice, his natural inclination was to focus on its source. He shifted around to see the small prayer vigil happening on the side of the road but was only able to catch a glimpse of the gathering before he felt a hard and unrelenting blow to the back of his head. Jacob had regained his bearings and started unleashing a barrage of heavy strikes on Richard's body.

Chapter 35

A caravan of military vehicles and one familiar government-issued car invaded the small downtown street just as Jacob threw Richard to the ground. Jacob had a strong hold of both Richard's arms as he lay face down on the pavement gritting his teeth. The pain still echoed in his head as he grunted and squirmed to get free. The scene reminded him of the highway incident and the police chase that followed. Despite the chill in the air, his body was covered in sweat and dirt, and his eyes were tightly shut as the pain emanated in his head.

George and Tom parked a safe distance from the scene and hurried on foot to get closer. General Corbin's men surrounded Jacob and Richard from all sides. They were all decked out in military gear, so it was hard to distinguish them from each other. Jackson was recognizable as he ran toward the scene carrying what looked like an oxygen mask with a small bottle attached to it. The General was right behind him though not keeping in step as he was too old and distinguished to run.

Jacob still had Richard pinned to the ground, and the circle of men around them had guns drawn ready to fire. Jackson burst through the circle and landed on his knees right at Richard's face.

Jacob kept his tight hold on Richard as Jackson pressed the mask close to Richard's face. The clear mask turned opaque as the yellow gas filled the chamber and entered Richard's lungs.

Richard began flailing as if he were choking on the substance. He was gasping and squirming relentlessly for what seemed like minutes. His eyes were wide open, and his face was struck with panic. Suddenly the movement stopped, and he was still. With the last breath of the deadly gas, Richard closed his eyes and succumbed to death. Jackson removed the mask and immediately covered Richard's face with a plastic film to contain the remains of the toxin that left a foamy residue on his lifeless mouth.

Jacob felt the limpness of Richard's arms. As he let go, those arms that had inflicted a bombardment of wounds on his body fell heavy on the ground. Jacob was sweaty, dirty and weary. He stammered to his feet and immediately began to get his bearings and look for Christina. Stewart and two other soldiers pointed their weapons at Jacob and ordered him to stay right there. Jacob was bruised and battered. He ignored their orders and walked past Stewart shoving him slightly as he passed. As soon as his eyes locked on Christina, he ran toward her as fast as he could. He was aching all over and ran with a limp, but he was undeterred in reaching his bride.

Christina's face was bright with relief as Jacob rushed to her and embraced her. They looked in each other's eyes and communicated volumes of emotion without ever saying a word.

George turned his attention and direction to Jacob and Christina while Tom maneuvered his way through the crowd keeping his focus on Richard's lifeless body still laying on the ground. The look of horror overcame Tom's face as he inched closer to the scene. Richard's eyes were closed and limp. His face was pale and motionless. Tom stopped in shock only a few feet from his body. The General was standing over Richard examining his handy work while several of his soldiers were still poised with guns aimed at Richard's lifeless body. The General reached for the side of his belt and grabbed the handgun strapped to his side. Tom glanced up at him in disbelief as he aimed the pistol at Richard and fired. Seven shots rang out one right after the other. Richard's body jolted slightly with each shot but was otherwise motionless. Each bullet bounced off his body and ricocheted onto some of the surrounding soldiers. The senseless act of macho superiority did nothing but feed the General's ego.

"What are you doing?" Tom yelled with his focus on the General. It was too late. The General had his agenda and his methods already planned out. He didn't answer but looked straight into Tom's eyes with a glare of harshness. He then focused his orders on the surrounding soldiers.

"Get this cleaned up," he said as he holstered his weapon and walked away from the scene. His men quickly went into action scurrying around like ants to contain and clean up the situation. Tom stood still in astonishment and disbelief as he was trying to process what he had just witnessed. This was not the way Tom had envisioned his final meeting with Richard. He stood still as the flurry of activity happened around him. As suddenly as the incident began, it was over.

George used his political influence to keep the General and his men away from Jacob. The General knew that George could cause him a great deal of stress if he got too specific about Corbin's tactics in his final report. They came to some mutually beneficial agreement behind closed doors, and the military presence at the scene quickly faded to nothing.

The remainder of the day seemed surreal to everyone involved. The military seized Richard's body. George asked Tom to stay on the scene until everything stabilized while he accompanied Jacob and Christina back home.

Chapter 36

George stayed with the Monroe family for a few days to help comfort them through the recovery process. He delayed the chip implant procedure to give Jacob's body some time to heal and stabilize after the incident. Tom buried himself in analysis reports and detailed documentation files. The General and his men demobilized from their home base, and Tom was glad to be rid of them. He kept tight hold of a bitter attitude toward the General and wouldn't talk to him or even acknowledge him after he intentionally had Richard killed.

Shortly after Tom and George had left Athens, Dagger was so distraught that he jumped out of his fifth floor hospital window and died instantly. When Tom heard the news, he wondered if Dagger ever realized that Tom lied to him or if he had just given up hope in life.

When George returned, he had lined up several meetings to debrief leadership and discuss next steps. Tom was able to use those meetings to validate his point that society needs some type of monitoring department. Naturally, everyone they talked to wanted more time to review and take the data into consideration, but Tom was confident that this chain of events would lead him back into the work he loved and back into a position of importance.

Jacob and Christina took some more time off work to recuperate from the trauma they had endured. George helped to work their situation with their respective employers and compensated them accordingly so they could focus on putting their lives back together.

Jacob healed quickly considering the amount of injury he sustained. Christina was only physically bruised but endured some emotional wounds that would take time to heal. The stress of the events kept her from getting solid rest at night. During the day, she would often sit in her wheelchair on the front porch and stare out into the countryside.

Six weeks after the incident as Christina was perched on the front porch, Jacob approached her from behind with a familiar red dress in his arms.

"Oh Jacob," Christina said with tears welling up in her eyes, "I thought that dress was ruined in the accident."

"It was. Mom helped me find an exact replacement, and I thought you'd like to wear it tonight."

The sweet grin that had been hidden too long once again appeared on Christina's face. "What's going on?" she said with a hint of excitement in her voice.

"We need to redeem our anniversary dinner."

The excitement beamed through her face, and the tears slowed ran down her cheeks.

"Really? Oh, Jacob that would be so…. wait, it takes weeks o get reservations at Baldomeros."

"I pulled some strings. We have dinner reservations at six."

Christina reached for his arm and pulled him close. "Thank you," she whispered as they embraced.

The evening played out similar to their first attempt. This time they borrowed Suzanna's car, and they both dressed in their finest clothes. As Christina rolled out the front door, Jacob already had the car door open and was standing ready to carry her to the vehicle. He gingerly placed her in the passenger seat and just beside her a worn and weathered photo album was waiting for her.

She immediately picked up the album and began studying the pictures as Jacob entered the car.

"Thank you again, sweetheart," she said with her focus on the pictures, "this was such a great idea and I'm so glad you remembered the photo album."

"I thought this would be a good way to start over."

"I am so happy to be your wife," Christina said still focused on the album. She studied each picture and turned the pages with her right hand while her left hand reached out for his.

"Oh, no," she said with a bit of sadness in her tone.

"What's wrong?"

"Our hiking picture. It's one of my favorites. It much have gotten lost."

"I'm sorry, Chrissy. I guess we'll have to go make another one."

"That may be a bit harder to do now," Christina said bringing their joined hands to touch her leg.

"If I have to, I'll carry you all across Stone Mountain," Jacob said with a reassuring smile.

They arrived at the restaurant safe and sound. Baldomeros was small but elegant and offered the finest dining in the area. They were seated at a table small enough that they could hold hands while they waited on their dinner. Christina proudly brought her weathered photo album into the restaurant, and they reminisced about all that they had been through. The night was perfect, and for the first time in weeks, they were able to count their blessings and feel comfortable with the life they had together.

The following Monday morning Jacob awoke early and quietly dressed as Christina slept. Just before he left their bedroom, Christina stirred and opened her eyes.

"Where are you going, sweetheart?"

"I've got a couple of errands to run. I'll be back by lunch," he said walking to her bedside. "I love you and I'll see you soon." He bent down and kissed her forehead before leaving for his mission.

Jacob hopped in his truck and drove to the local junkyard where Christina's wrecked car was towed after the accident.

Jacob asked the man at the front desk about the car, and he pointed Jacob in the right direction. After a few minutes of searching, Jacob found their damaged vehicle sitting in a row of other compact cars that had been wrecked or stripped for parts.

He whispered a little prayer under his breath and began searching for Christina's special picture that he wished was still somewhere in the car's interior. He lost hope at first as he searched the floorboards and seat pockets, but his faith was restored when he reached under the passenger seat to feel a dried thick piece of paper. A smile overcame him as he pulled it out to discover the treasure he had come for.

Feeling confident in his discovery, Jacob extracted himself from the driver's side of the car and closed the door. He started to walk away, but an odd reflection of the sun caught his attention. Jacob walked slowly toward the mangled front left wheel well of the car with a perplexed look on his face. The reflection had passed as clouds began to fill the sky. Upon closer examination he found the remains of a small shiny box no larger than his hand. Jacob didn't know what it was, but he knew enough about cars to know that this particular part didn't belong there. He reached in the wheel well and pulled on the box. Still having his strength, the box came loose without much effort. As he examined it, he noticed that it had once contained a small electronic circuit and had shards of metal on the inside. It appeared that the box had been punctured, but not from the outside. It had exploded from the inside resulting in a hole about the size of a quarter.

Jacob's mind was racing as all of the parts of the puzzle began coming together in his head. His emotion ranged from perplexed to shock. As he continued to think about the events and conversations of the past few weeks, his breath became quick and heavy. He thought about the accident and the timing of George and Tom's visit. He remembered Tom's request before he and George left his parent's house. He recalled the fight with Richard in the street of downtown Griffin and remembered seeing Christina helpless on the curb. His face became hot and red as anger built from within him. He crushed what was left of the small box and let it drop to the ground. He kept a steady glare on his face as he walked out of the junkyard and back to his truck with a picture in one hand and a fire in his eyes.

As he approached the truck, Jacob pulled his phone from the back pocket of his jeans to make a call.

"Dad, I need to get an address and a phone number from you please..."

Chapter 37

Tom Marshall Monitor Log Personal File AJHN316

My cell phone rang at exactly 10:00am while I was at my desk in my office tidying up some reports. George had asked to meet with me that afternoon. He wanted to review some of the final documentation we were preparing for the leadership report. After countless meetings and weeks of debates and depositions, there was a renewed interest in people of my skill set in top government positions. I felt like I should have been happier, but something was gnawing at me from the inside. My own internal unrest was amplified by the strengthening storm outside. It was the time of year for nasty weather, but this particular storm was much more ominous than normal. The clouds were thick, and the wind was furious. The knot in my stomach grew tense as I grabbed my cell phone without looking at the caller ID.

"Hello, this is Tom," I said trying to act normal. I was expecting the call to be from George. The tone of the voice on the other end of the line rattled me.

"Tom, what have you done?"

It was Jacob. There was an undertone of anger in his voice "Answer me, Tom".

"Um, Jacob, what are you talking about? Are you okay?" I said still trying to play off ignorance.

"Your game is over, Tom. I know what you did. I know what you did to my Chrissy. Where are you?"

For the first time in my life, Jacob's voice struck fear to my very core. He knew. How did he know? My mind was racing. I didn't have a plan for this. I felt exposed and panicked. I silently waited not knowing what to say until I heard a click on the phone, and I knew that our conversation was over. I rushed out of my office, down the hall, and out the front door to my car. The rain was cold and heavy. It pelted my body as I ran toward my car fumbling for my keys.

Jacob was coming for me. He was coming with a vengeance, and I had nowhere to run. I had stirred a beast with great power, and I was clearly the object of his wrath. The fear gripped me and reminded me of my ordeal in the back of the moving truck with Richard. I knew an encounter with Jacob would be different. Richard didn't know the part I played in this grand scheme. The tone of Jacob's voice clearly communicated that he did. He knew that I had taken something from him, and for the first time in my life, I realized that I deserved what was coming.

I drove home as quickly as I could in the pouring rain. I sprinted to the front door locking it behind me but knowing that the deadbolt lock wasn't going to keep me safe if I was still here when Jacob showed up. I quickly grabbed my travel suitcase and stuffed it with clothes hoping for a speedy getaway. I didn't know where to go, but I knew I had to leave. If I could just get away, I could start over somewhere. I could keep avoiding the conviction of my actions. The knot in my gut became huge, and the sweat was dripping from my brow. Just as I finished zipping up my suitcase, I heard the bang on the front door.

"Oh, God," I said to myself with a shaky voice.

"Open the door, Tom," Jacob said as he rapped heavy on the door still holding back his fury.

I abandoned my suitcase and bolted for the back door. As soon as he saw my shadow through the small window next to the front door, Jacob burst through the door leaving the shattered remains behind him. His strength was in full force, and he left broken furniture in his wake as he chased me out the back door.

I made it past the back porch but tripped on a chair and fell face first in the center of my small backyard. The ground was mushy, and the front side of my body was covered in mud. The rain had softened, but the sky was still filled with dark clouds and the occasional lightning bolt. I turned around to see Jacob towering over me ready to strike. I could almost feel his hot angry breath on my face.

269

"Please Jacob, let me...."

"Let you what?" Jacob said. His voice was harsh and there was rage in his eyes. "Let you tell me why you crippled my wife? Let you tell me why you killed my baby?"

"Oh, God," I said too scared to mutter any other words.

"Don't you dare!" Jacob replied, "Don't you dare call out to God now. You spent a lifetime denying God and now you want to cry out to him when you're about to die?"

"Please don't kill me, Jacob," I murmured as I laid on the ground helpless.

"Tell me how you did it, Tom." My failure to reply stimulated Jacob's low harsh voice to become a shout. "Tell me!"

"Ok." I was shaking uncontrollably. The terror brought tears to my eyes and made my voice shaky and sheepish. "Richard was out of control. Things weren't going like I planned. I needed someone who could beat him. When you refused to help, I had to find a way to pull you in. I didn't think I could do it without you. Richard captured me. I told him that Flint Chemical had a medicine that would fix his headaches. I told him that they were testing it at the pharmaceutical lab in Griffin. I told him that Christina was the lab technician who could give it to him. I didn't mean for anyone to get hurt. I didn't know about your baby. I didn't know about..."

"That's enough, Tom. You are nothing but a worm. You would sacrifice the lives and happiness of others for your own agenda. How many people are you willing to hurt?"

"Please don't kill me, Jacob." I whined like a schoolboy being scolded by the principal.

"Give me a good reason not to."

"I... I don't want to lose my life."

"Life. What life?"

I was silent.

"I'm not going to kill you, Tom," Jacob said as he stood up straight. His voice was harsh. His eyes were hard, but the anger was subsiding. "I pity you, Tom. More than any other man, I pity you. My mom and dad lost their little girl. My wife lost her ability to walk. We lost our baby before he was even born. My family knows what loss is, and now you're begging for a life that you lost a long time ago. Our normal lives were taken from us, but you gave yours up; and for what? A weekly paycheck and a false sense of power. You are a pitiful man, Tom Marshall. You are nothing but a pitiful man afraid of losing a life you never really had," Jacob said as he shook his head side to side.

The mud soaked though my clothes as I lay there listening and crying. I had curled up in a fetal position anticipating Jacob's blows. I was soaked and dirty from head to toe as Jacob towered over me with the power and the motive to end my degenerate life. Then Jacob took a deep breath and just turned away.

"We're done," he said and he started walking back toward the porch. "Leave us alone from now on."

He walked back through the house and out through what was left of the front door. Even after he was gone I laid in that mud hole paralyzed with fear, regret, and emptiness.

"You're right, Jacob," I said with no one around to hear. "It was all my fault. It wasn't just Jacob and Christina's baby. It was everything. I was on flight 828 from Atlanta to New York. The plane crash wasn't an accident. I used my training, my security access and my position to sabotage the airplane that Richard Hall was on. I knew right where to hit him. I shattered his restrainer chip. I let the power within him loose so that I could regain my job and life I knew. People on that plane died because of me. I orchestrated the car crash that crippled Christina and killed her baby. I took advantage of every person and every opportunity to make myself feel better. Richard wasn't any worse than me. He manipulated people and events to get what he wanted; so did I. His selfish disregard for others led to tragedy; so did mine. Richard's selfishness drew public attention; mine was a hidden destroyer. Jacob was right; I am only a worm.

I sat up, lowered my head, and combed my fingers through my dirty hair. I could taste the salt from my tears on my lips. I took a deep breath and continued my confession.

"Because of me, eleven people on Flight 828 died. Because of me, Officer Davis was hit by a truck and died. Because of me, Jacob and Christina lost their first child. Because of me, Christina can't walk again." I took another deep breath as the full realization of what I had done hit me like a brick. "I lied to Dagger and gave him false hope. I let him believe that I cared about him, and then I betrayed him. I used Christina as a pawn so I could manipulate Jacob to clean up my mess. I watched from the side lines as they fought in the street, and I watched as the General and his men delivered the final blow to Richard."

I sat in the mud, sobbing like a small child. I remembered how I thought I had everything I wanted. I got my job and my reputation back, but at a price that I could not repay. I got what I asked for, but I am so lost, so empty, and so wretched. What kind of a man am I? In that very moment, I wished Jacob had killed me. Why didn't he? Why would God even let me be born? Why wouldn't God himself strike me down?

The pain in my gut was wrenching. My whole body was still trembling. The ache of my heart was unbearable. I wanted to die. "Oh, God", I cried, "I am so evil. I have destroyed so much. I have ruined so many lives. I am ruined. I am such a waste... Is there anything but

misery and destruction for a man as wicked as me? Is there any hope?"

After that, I could speak no longer. I couldn't stop weeping. My

actions were despicable. I just sat there on the ground with my eyes

clenched shut and my face buried in my hands. In my head I kept

repeating that last phrase, *"is there any hope?"* Seconds went by. The rain

stopped, and my wet hair dripped water into my lap. Suddenly there

was no noise. Eerie silence consumed me for a few seconds. Then I felt

a small breeze across my face. It was then that I heard it- a small voice

no louder than the tiniest whisper but clear as daylight.

"There is...."

Tom Marshall Monitor Log Personal File AJN316
End of record

Coming next in the series:

Revelation of the Elite

Made in the USA
Columbia, SC
18 December 2020